Ratsey raised the weapon he was carrying and fired. . . .

It was a harquebus, a type of musket. Tom had never seen such a thing before, never heard anything as loud as the explosion it made. At first he wasn't even sure what had happened. It seemed to him that Hawkins had thrown his own weapon away. Then the traveler turned, and to Tom's horror there was a great hole in the center of his chest and blood was pouring out, soaking down into his trousers, draining out of him even as Tom watched. Behind him Ratsey had lowered his gun and was muttering something, but Tom, his ears still ringing, couldn't hear him. Smoke curled up from the muzzle of the harquebus. Hawkins staggered toward him.

"To London," he rasped. "Go to Moorfield...."

AN ALA BEST BOOK FOR YOUNG ADULTS

BOOKS BY ANTHONY HOROWITZ

The Devil and His Boy

THE ALEX RIDER ADVENTURES
Stormbreaker
Point Blank
Skeleton Key
Eagle Strike
Scorpia
Ark Angel

THE DIAMOND BROTHERS MYSTERIES
Public Enemy Number Two
The Falcon's Malteser
Three of Diamonds
South by Southeast

ANTHONY HOROWITZ

The Devil and His Boy

PUFFIN BOOKS

For Wendy Boase

PUFFIN BOOKS
Published by the Penguin Group
Penguin Young Readers Group, 345 Hudson Street, New York, New York 10014, U.S.A.
Penguin Group (Canada), 90 Eglinton Avenue East, Suite 700, Toronto, Ontario, Canada M4P 2Y3
(a division of Pearson Penguin Canada Inc.)
Penguin Books Ltd, 80 Strand, London WC2R 0RL, England
Penguin Ireland, 25 St Stephen's Green, Dublin 2, Ireland (a division of Penguin Books Ltd)
Penguin Group (Australia), 250 Camberwell Road, Camberwell, Victoria 3124, Australia
(a division of Pearson Australia Group Pty Ltd)
Penguin Books India Pvt Ltd, 11 Community Centre, Panchsheel Park, New Delhi - 110 017, India
Penguin Group (NZ), Cnr Airborne and Rosedale Roads, Albany, Auckland 1310, New Zealand
(a division of Pearson New Zealand Ltd)
Penguin Books (South Africa) (Pty) Ltd, 24 Sturdee Avenue, Rosebank, Johannesburg 2196, South Africa

Registered Offices: Penguin Books Ltd, 80 Strand, London WC2R 0RL, England

Published in Great Britain by Walker Books Ltd., London, 1998
First published in the United States of America by Philomel Books,
a division of Penguin Putnam Books for Young Readers, 2000
Published by Puffin Books, a division of Penguin Putnam Books for Young Readers, 2001
This edition published by Puffin Books, a division of Penguin Young Readers Group, 2007

1 3 5 7 9 10 8 6 4 2

Copyright © Anthony Horowitz, 1998
All rights reserved

THE LIBRARY OF CONGRESS HAS CATALOGED THE PHILOMEL EDITION AS FOLLOWS:
Horowitz, Anthony, date.
The Devil and his boy / Anthony Horowitz.—1st American ed.
p. cm.
Summary: In 1593, thirteen-year-old Tom travels through the English countryside to London,
where he falls in with a troupe of actors and finds himself in great danger from several sources.
[1. Theater Fiction. 2. Adventure and adventurers Fiction.
3. London (England) Fiction. 4. England Fiction.] I. Title.
PZ7.H7875Dc 2000 [Fic]—dc21 99-39791 CIP
ISBN 0-399-23432-2

Puffin Books ISBN 978-0-14-240797-4

Printed in the United States of America

INTRODUCTION
❖

I hated history when I was at school.

This was largely the fault of my history teacher, Mr. Evans, who was so old that we often used to think that he must have been alive when most of it was happening. I still remember his terrible, whining voice... he used to speak as if he had dust at the back of his throat. And he never looked at us. To this day, I'm not sure if his eyes were real or made of glass, but as he sat, hunched up over his desk at the front of the classroom, he used to remind me of an exhibit in a museum. It really was as if someone had taken him to the taxidermist and got him stuffed before he was quite dead.

For Mr. Evans, history was just a series of names and dates that we all had to learn by heart. So a lesson might go...

1605	Gunpowder Plot
1618	Thirty Years War begins
1620	Pilgrim Fathers
1642	Civil War
1649	Execution of Charles I

And on. And on. And on...

It wasn't until I had left school that I began to think that history might have been more fun than Mr. Evans had ever have imagined. Take another look at the list above. The Gunpowder Plot could be a really exciting story about a bunch of Spanish spies who tunnel underneath the Houses of Parliament in London and try to blow the whole place up. And what about the Pilgrim Fathers who crossed the Atlantic in the Mayflower and landed in America? For them, it must have been an amazing journey across a world that was completely unknown. What was it like? How many of them got seasick? And I'd have loved to have been present at the execution of poor King Charles. The whole of London turned out to watch... but then in those days having your head chopped off was something of an entertainment.

By now you should be getting the general idea. *The Devil and His Boy* is a history story—but it's very much *my* sort of history. Basically, it's an adventure story that just happens to take place five hundred years ago.

I would have loved to have lived during the reign of Queen Elizabeth I. It was such a rude, noisy, dirty, dangerous, difficult time. London would have stank. There were no toilets and the sewage ran right down the middle of the streets. No wonder there were so many outbreaks of the plague. London was much, much smaller than it is now, surrounded by thick forests that were full of highwaymen—so even getting there safely was an achievement. And once you arrived, you couldn't expect to be welcomed with open arms. On the contrary, the Londoners were famous for their bad manners. Often they would throw mud balls (or worse) at visiting tourists just because they felt like it. There were thieves and tricksters everywhere. They'd take your luggage and your life.

If you had lived in London in the sixteenth century, you would have shared one room (and possibly one bed) with your mother, your father, your brothers and your sisters, and possibly a couple of pigs and a duck too. You almost certainly wouldn't go to school. And you might well be married before you were even thirteen. Not that it would be a long marriage. Most people died in their thirties...maybe that was why life was so intense.

There would be no TV, no computer games, and no books like this one—hardly anyone could read so why bother? But you'd be able to kick a pig's bladder around in the street—the beginning of soccer—or perhaps pop out to a nice public hanging. You would never, ever have a bath. And you would wear the same clothes until they either rotted away or burst. What a laugh!

And at the same time, you would be a citizen of a country that ruled the world. At this time, America was hardly known at all (and there was certainly nothing united about the states). Britain was at war with much of Europe, but, thanks to heroes like Sir Walter Raleigh and Sir Francis Drake, we always seemed to be on the winning side. And then there was Shakespeare! The world's greatest playwright was alive and working on the south bank of the River Thames. How I wish I could have been at the first night of *Hamlet* or *Macbeth*. If only I could have got his autograph ... just think what it would be worth now!

Anyway, it's time to get on with the book. I loved writing it. It was my first book to be published in the USA. And I still think it's a lot of fun... even if it is history.

Anthony Horowitz
Crouch End, London
July 2006

Contents

1

The Stone of Vision

It was just before midnight when Queen Elizabeth slipped out of bed and went in search of her magician.

Although she had allowed her ladies-in-waiting to lead her into the bedroom and help her undress more than an hour before, she hadn't even tried to sleep. Part of the trouble, of course, was being queen of England. She could still feel the crown on her head even when she wasn't wearing it. . . . There was so much to think about, so much to do. But the real problem was her bed. It was a huge, four-postered thing with no fewer than five quilts. The first was silk, the next velvet; then there was a gold one and a silver one and finally, on top, a quilt embroidered with a rather gloomy picture of the Sermon on the Mount. The quilts had been given to her by the Spanish ambassador, the French ambassador, the Dutch ambassador, the German ambassador, and the archbishop of Canterbury, and she had to use them all so that she did not give offense to any one of them. The result was that even on the coldest winter nights she was always much too hot.

For a moment she stood in the middle of the room and glanced out of the window. There was a full moon that night, which pleased the queen. She knew that the magician would like it. Somehow his spells always worked better when there was a moon, and this one seemed huge—a perfect white circle hanging in the darkness. Her eyes traveled down and she saw the Thames, ash white as it twisted through the city of London. Everything was silent. The queen nodded. This was the right time.

She crossed the room to a tapestry that covered an entire wall. The tapestry showed a lion being hunted, and when she was young, the snarling face with its ugly eyes had given her nightmares. But she was an elderly woman now. Sixty years old. And how could she have nightmares when she hardly ever slept?

The tapestry was suspended from a rail, and she pulled it aside to reveal a bare brick wall with no visible door or window. At the far end of the wall, over a bookshelf, there was a metal hook. Without hesitating, the queen went over to it and turned it. There was a click, and a whole section of the wall swung inward on a hidden hinge to reveal a jagged opening and a spiral staircase leading down. Gray cobwebs hung in the air. A fat black spider, frightened by the light from the bedroom, tumbled down the brickwork and then scuttled along the floor, disappearing into the shadows.

The queen lifted a candle from her room and started forward. After the warmth of the bedroom, the stairs were very cold. A draft twisted around her ankles and slithered up her legs. The candle in her hand flickered and her shadow seemed to jump away, tugging at her as if it could pull her back upstairs. For a moment she wondered if this was a good idea. She could still turn back, go to bed, and forget all about it. The queen was afraid. But she remembered now what she had done—what she had been forced to do—exactly forty years ago. Forty years of silence! It was time for it to end.

She continued down. A moth, attracted by the light, flew into her face. Its feathery wings brushed against her lips and she gasped out loud. Her hand banged against the wall and she almost dropped the candle. She stopped for a minute, catching her breath. Then, gripping the candle more tightly, she followed the stairs to their end, passing through an archway and along a corridor where the ceiling curved low over her head, as if groaning under the weight of the great palace a hundred yards above.

She had reached a door made of thick planks of wood bound together with iron and so low that she had to bend to open it. It reminded her of the door of one of her own dungeons. Her hand found a silver ring and she turned it, the metal cold against her skin. On the other side a warm yellow glow and the faint smell of rosemary welcomed her into a small, circular chamber. The door swung shut behind her as she went in.

"Good evening, Queen."

"You were expecting me, Wizard?"

"Oh, yes. I knew you intended to visit me before you had even decided it yourself. Sit down. . . ."

Nobody else would have dared to talk to Queen Elizabeth in this way. For a start, she could have been called "Your Royal Highness" or "Your Majesty." And nobody ever told her what to do—not even so much as to sit down. But the person seated in the high, wood-backed chair was no ordinary man.

Dr. John Dee was sixty-six years old but looked much older, having a white mustache and a white beard that came to a point about halfway down his chest. He wore a long black robe and a black cap that could have been painted onto his head. His eyes were brown, a strange, watery brown, the color of melted chocolate. There was a gray cat, half-asleep, on his lap, and he occasionally stroked it with a long, elegant finger. Dr. Dee spoke with a Welsh accent. So, rather more remarkably, did the cat.

"You know why I have come," the queen said.

"Of course I do."

"Do you know everything, Wizard?"

Dr. Dee shook his head. "I know many things, Queen, and my stone of vision tells me more, but only God knows everything. I am just a man."

"Can you tell me when I am going to die?" the queen asked.

The magician hesitated. His eyes narrowed and he seemed unsure what to say. Then the cat arched its back, stretched its legs, and suddenly opened its quite brilliant emerald eyes. "You will die," the cat said, "when you stop breathing."

There was a silence in the room. For a long minute the queen gazed at the cat. Then she smiled. "It is a good answer," she said.

"But that is not the question you came to ask," Dr. Dee muttered.

"No." Suddenly the queen was nervous. Her fingers closed on a gold locket she was wearing around her neck. She had taken off all her other jewelry for bed. But this locket never left her. It was part of her. "I wish to know about him," she said.

"Why now?"

"Today is his birthday." She fell silent for a moment, then said, "I think of him all the time, Wizard. I know I can never see him, but I still wonder about him—whether he is dead or alive."

Dr. Dee stroked the cat. "I can tell you what you

want to know," he said. "But I have to warn you now, Queen. It might be better not to ask. Magic has a nasty way of changing things. You cast a spell, you ask for secret knowledge, and before you know it, you have opened a barrel of worms . . . or perhaps something worse than worms."

"I still have to know," the queen insisted. "Enough of this, Wizard. You have known me long enough to know when my mind is made up. Do your magic. Tell me what you see."

"She's making a mistake," the cat murmured.

"Hush!" Dr. Dee stroked the cat, then lifted it up and set it to one side.

There was a low table between Dr. Dee and the queen with a number of objects scattered across the top. These were the tools of the magician's trade. There were three or four old books, so old that the words seemed to be sinking into the thick, yellowish pages. There were two candles and a tapering wand. Between them lay what looked like an ordinary piece of silvery-gray stone about the size of a dinner plate. Dr. Dee picked it up and cradled it in his hands.

"I will need something of his," Dr. Dee said in a low voice.

Once again the queen's fingers reached for the locket around her neck, but this time she took it and drew it over her head. Nestling it in the palm of one hand, she opened it with the other. Inside the locket was the miniature portrait of a man, and opposite it, a lock of light brown hair. The queen gazed at the hair for what seemed like an eternity, then let it fall onto the table. "It is all that I have," she said.

"Are you prepared to lose it?"

There was a flicker of anger in the queen's eyes. "Do what you have to," she said.

Dr. Dee picked up the hair and laid it on the stone. He cupped his hands around the stone without touching it, his eyes fixed on the stone as if he were trying to look through it. The queen leaned forward, and as she did so, the lock of hair moved. She thought that it had been caught in a draft, but then she realized that the stone had become hot and that it was the heat that was causing the effect. The air above the stone was shimmering. The color of the stone was changing: from gray to white, and then to metallic silver.

"No . . . !" The word escaped the queen's lips as a gasp. The lock of hair had burst into flame. Now the flickering pieces rose into the air, twisted, and disappeared. The surface of the stone was no longer rough or remotely stony. It had become a mirror, but as Dr. Dee looked into it, it did not show his reflection.

"His name was Robert." The magician's eyes were focused in the distance, and the queen knew that he was seeing things outside the room, outside and far away.

"Yes. Robert. . . ." Even uttering his name was a knife-wound. She had never done it before. "Tell me, Wizard. Is he alive?"

A long silence. And then . . .

"No, Queen. He is dead."

The queen fell back in her chair, covering her eyes with her hands. Somehow she had always expected it, but like all bad news it had lost none of its power to hurt. Dr. Dee was still gazing into the mirror that had been a stone, and there was a look of puzzlement on his face.

"What is it?" the queen demanded.

"I don't know. . . ." And then, as if a cloud had parted and the sun had broken through, the magician looked up. "He had a son," he said.

"What?"

"Robert is dead, but his son is still alive."

The queen gripped the sides of her chair. "Where is he? What is he called? What do you know about him?"

"He is far from here. I cannot see his name." The stone was getting hotter and hotter. The very air inside the chamber was beginning to burn.

"Try! You must try!"

"No. All I can see is a castle and a pig. It is difficult. . . ." Dr. Dee waved a hand over the stone, clearing the smoke. "The pig is outside the castle and over the boy."

"He is still a boy? How old is he?"

"Thirteen. The castle—" Dr. Dee frowned. "They are building chimneys on the castle. Strange-looking chimneys. I can see the boy limping past the castle and he's looking at the chimneys and . . ."

"Why is he limping?"

"Because of the pig . . ."

"Why must your answers be so mysterious, Wizard? Where is the boy? If you can't tell me his name, at least tell me where he is!"

But before Dr. Dee could reply, there was a sudden crackle like a musket going off. At the same time the mirror shattered, a thousand cracks exploding across its surface. Then the cracks faded and a second later the stone was exactly as it had been, lying flat and ordinary on the table.

"That is all I can tell you, Queen." Dr. Dee picked up the stone. It was quite cool to the touch. "But you have spies and men of intelligence. It should be enough."

"A castle, strange chimneys, and a pig. Another of your wretched riddles, Wizard. Where do I even start?"

"Framlingham!" The cat—which had been quite forgotten during all this—leapt onto Dr. Dee's lap. "They're building chimneys on Framlingham Castle."

"How do you know?" the queen asked.

The cat shrugged. "A little bird told me," it remarked. "And then I ate the little bird."

"Framlingham . . . in Suffolk." The queen got to her

feet. "Only four or five days from here. You have done well, Wizard. You have my thanks and will have much more!"

The queen left, climbing back up the secret staircase to her bedroom. She was still awake when the sun rose above the thatched roofs and wooden houses of London and the first horses stumbled along the rough, pitted tracks that were the city's roads. The year was 1593. The queen, of course, was Elizabeth I. And she was already planning the course of events that would change one boy's life forever, and with it the entire history of the country she ruled.

2

The Pig's Head

It was raining in Framlingham: a cold, gray December rain that dripped and trickled into every corner and wiped away the color of everything it touched. The streets were so full of puddles that there were more puddles than street, with only a few patches of brown mud here and there to remind you that the place had once been built on dry land. The two moats surrounding Framlingham Castle were full to overflowing. The town gardens and bowling green had disappeared.

The inn stood just outside the town, next to a large swamp. It was a squat, dark, evil-smelling place with rotting timbers and moldy walls. It had few windows—glass was too expensive—but the noise of singing and the smell of roasting meat seeped through the thatched roof and chimney. An inn sign swung in the wind. The sign showed the head of a pig, severed from its body, for that was the inn's name:

THE PIG'S HEAD, FRAMLINGHAM.

PROPRIETORS: SEBASTIAN & HENRIETTA SLOPE.

At about five o'clock in the afternoon a young boy came out of the inn carrying a bucket. Despite the weather, he was wearing only the lightest of clothes: a shirt open at the neck, a waistcoat that was too short for him, a pair of trousers that flapped around his ankles. He had neither shoes nor socks. His bare feet splashed in the mud as he went to draw water from the well.

The boy was about twelve or thirteen years old. Nobody knew or cared exactly when he had been born. He had long reddish-brown hair, pale skin, and bright, intelligent blue eyes. He was painfully thin—his rags seemed to hang off his shoulders without actually touching his body—and there was a bruise on the side of his cheek the size of a man's fist. He lowered the bucket into the well, gripping the handle that groaned rustily as it turned; his fingers were unusually long and slender. The boy's name was Thomas Falconer. That, at least, would be the name they'd carve on his gravestone when starvation or the plague carried him away. For now they simply called him Tom.

He was about to lift the bucket out of the well when a sound made him turn. A man had appeared, a traveler on horseback, his body lost in the folds of a dark cloak, his face hidden by his hat. The horse was a great black stallion with a white blaze on its chest. Steam was snorting from its nostrils as it jerked forward, its hooves striking angrily in the mud. It came to a halt, and the rider swung himself effortlessly down. Mud had splattered his brown leather boots and the bottom of his cloak. He had evidently been riding for some time.

"Boy!" the man called out.

Forgetting the bucket, Tom ran forward to obey. "Yes, my lord?"

"Take the horse to the stable. See that he's watered and fed. If any harm comes to him, you'll answer for it."

The man dragged his luggage from behind his saddle and handed the reins to Tom. He was about to turn away, but suddenly he stopped, and for a moment Tom found himself being examined by two narrow gray eyes in a dark, weathered face.

"What is your name, boy?" the man demanded.

"Tom, my lord." Tom was surprised. People seldom took any notice of him.

"How long have you worked here, Tom?"

"All my life, my lord. Ever since I was able to work."

The rider stared at Tom as if trying to read something in his face. "Your parents own this building?" he asked.

Tom shook his head. "My parents are dead," he said.

"Who were they? Do you know?"

It was one question too many. Travelers often passed through Framlingham on their way to the ports at Harwich and Ipswich, but they came as strangers and that was how they left. It was the unwritten law. In an uncertain world, it could be dangerous to give too much information about yourself.

Tom's lips clamped shut. The man seemed to understand. "Take care of the horse, Tom," he said, and walked into the inn.

The inn was crowded, the fire a distant red glimmer behind so many huddled bodies. Thick smoke coiled upward from the hearth, from the tallow candles on the mantel, and from pipes clenched in the teeth of men and women too. Two more boys—older and better fed than Tom—were bustling in and out of the kitchen carrying wooden trenchers of meat and bread, somehow forcing their way through the great tangle to find the tables beyond. Someone somewhere was playing a fiddle, but the sound was almost drowned out by the shouting, arguing, laughing, and drunken singing of the guests.

The landlord noticed the new arrival the moment the door opened, but then he had the sort of eyes that noticed everything. This was Sebastian Slope. He was a small, nervous man who had never quite recovered from the pox that had ravaged his skin and eaten away part of his nose. He had tried to grow a beard and mustache to hide the damage, but unfortunately the hair—as well as being bright orange—was thin and uneven, sprouting in one part of his face but not in another, with the result that he looked as if he had been horribly injured—perhaps by a musket at close range.

Rubbing his pale white hands together, he approached the new arrival, who was standing there waiting, water dripping from his cloak.

"Good evening, my lord. Welcome. Welcome to The Pig's Head." Slope's teeth had long ago rotted away—all but a couple of them—and he now found it easier to speak through what was left of his nose. His voice was thin and high-pitched. If a rat could talk, it would probably sound much the same. "What can I fetch for you, my lord? A pint of the finest ale? A delicious supper? A nice leg of mutton? Or perhaps the speciality of the house. A potato! Have you ever tried a potato, my lord? It is quite new and the most remarkable thing. . . ."

"I need a room for the night," the traveler interrupted.

"Of course. Of course. We can provide you with the best linen sheets. And only six of our guests have slept on them since they were last washed. . . ."

"I'll have a bed with clean sheets. And I'll eat some lamb. Yes. And a rabbit too. Mushrooms. Some cheese. And beer, not ale."

"Beer. Yes. Yes. Will you have the meal in your chamber, my lord, or at the common table? It'll be sixpence downstairs and eightpence up, but if you have it up perhaps we could arrange for one of our kitchen maids to keep you company . . . ?" Slope twisted half his face into a secretive smile and winked so many times that it looked as if his eye might fall out.

The stranger frowned. "I'll eat down here."

"You do us all a privilege and a joy, my lord." Slope smiled, but at the same time a strange gleam had come into his eyes so that he looked both servile and sinister at the same time. "Have you come far, my lord?"

"From London," the stranger replied.

"And returning soon?"

"Tomorrow."

This was the information that the innkeeper had been angling for. He swallowed once, his Adam's apple performing a somersault in his scrawny throat. "Henrietta!" he called out. "Henny!"

A moment later a tiny woman with gray, straggly hair hurried out of the smoke. This was Henrietta Slope, and although to look at she could have been Sebastian's grandmother, she was in fact his wife. She too had caught the pox—in seventeen years' marriage it was the only thing her husband had given her. The disease had attacked her lips, which had shriveled away so that when she smiled she was forced to use her teeth.

"We have a guest," Sebastian said.

"A guest! How lovely! And a gentleman!" Henrietta

curtsied twice. "Have you ordered food, my lord? The food here is a delight. We have only had nine cases of food poisoning since our new cook started. . . ."

"I've ordered," the traveler muttered.

"He has indeed," Sebastian agreed. "Lamb. Mushrooms. Cheese. And rabbit. . . ."

"Rabbit?" Henrietta grinned liplessly. "Fresh today. It couldn't be fresher. In fact, I strangled it myself."

"Thank you." The traveler seemed to be in a hurry to get away from this odd couple, but suddenly he leaned across the bar and drew them closer to him. "I was speaking just now to that boy outside . . ." he began.

"Tom?" Sebastian's face darkened. "If he offended your lordship, I'll throw him down the well."

"That boy's useless!" Henrietta shrieked. "He's worse than useless. He's a drip. He's a damp patch. A dead worm!"

"He hasn't offended me," the traveler interrupted. "I am merely interested in him. Where did you find him?"

Sebastian glanced at his wife, then leered at the new guest. "Are you interested in buying him?" he asked.

"We might sell him," Henrietta simpered. "Although of course we'd miss him. He works very well for us. A very hard worker. Very fit." She seemed to have completely forgotten what she had been saying only a few moments before.

"Where did you find him?"

"He was an orphan." Henrietta's eyes filled with tears. "I have two sons of my own, my lord. I took him in out of the goodness of my heart." She tapped her chest, which seemed too thin and hollow to contain any heart at all. "We look after him in return for a few light tasks about the house. . . ."

"What of his parents?" the traveler asked, becoming more interested by the second.

"They worked up at the castle," Sebastian replied. "The father fell off a horse and broke his neck. The mother died giving birth to him. He came into the world with nothing, and but for Mrs. S. and myself, nothing is all he'd have now."

The traveler's eyes narrowed, and for a moment he said nothing. He was obviously deep in thought. But then he shook his head and straightened up. "Send me my food as soon as possible," he said, and went and sat at the nearest table.

Sebastian Slope watched the man as he took his place, then slipped through a door and into the kitchen. Here there was a second, huge fire with a rather angry-looking pig on a spit being turned by a fat, sweating cook with dirty hands and a runny nose. Henrietta had followed her husband in and now he drew her to one side, standing over a huge cauldron of soup that was slowly congealing.

"What do you think, my precious?" he asked.

"Rich," Henrietta murmured. "Definitely rich."

"So I thought." Sebastian tried to pick his nose, remembered it wasn't there, and bit his nail absentmindedly instead. "Did you notice the cloak lined with velvet, my jewel? And the boots. . . ."

Henrietta nodded. "I think this is one for Ratsey," she muttered.

"Yes," Sebastian said. "Ratsey will like this one. You had better summon the boy."

But at that very moment the outer door opened and Tom came back into the kitchen. It had begun to rain more heavily and water dripped out of his hair, running down the side of his neck. He was carrying the bucket, full now and heavy.

"Where have you been?" Sebastian swung a lazy arm and slapped the back of his hand across Tom's head.

"Lazing again, I'll be bound!" Henrietta swung her arm, too, only harder.

"I'm sorry!" Tom cried out. "A gentleman came. He told me to see to his horse."

"Yes." Sebastian leaned closer. Tom cowered away, but the landlord was smiling. "What sort of a horse does he ride?"

"A stallion. Black with a white mark."

"Valuable?"

Tom hesitated. He knew what was about to happen

and thought about lying, but it was no good. The Slopes would know. They always did. "Yes," he said.

Sebastian grabbed him by the collar and drew him so close that his lips almost touched the boy's ear. "You're to go into the wood," he whispered. "Find Ratsey. Tell him we have a mark. The London road. Tomorrow."

"But it's dark. It's raining. . . ."

"Are you arguing with me?" Sebastian hadn't raised his voice but his grip had tightened and his eyes, dark to begin with, had gone almost black.

"No, Master Slope."

"Then be off with you. To the burnt oak. And if he isn't there, wait for him to come."

Tom ran out, slamming the door behind him. Sebastian and Henrietta Slope watched him go.

"You're too kind to that child," Henrietta sighed.

"I am softhearted, I know it," Sebastian agreed.

"I wonder why our guest was so interested in him?" Henrietta scratched her head and sighed as a lump of hair fell into the soup. Her disease was definitely getting worse.

Sebastian considered for a moment. "I suppose we'll never know," he replied.

Husband and wife kissed each other, gray lipless teeth onto gray pockmarked flesh. Then they left the kitchen and went back into the inn.

3

Gamaliel Ratsey

After he had left The Pig's Head, Tom climbed up the hill and back into the town center. It had stopped raining and the clouds had parted enough to allow a slice of moonlight to cut through. Tom was grateful for it. Without the moon he would have had to make the journey in almost pitch blackness, for the only other light came from the candles burning behind the windows of the houses, and with the high price of wax, there were few enough of them.

He passed through the market square, skirting around an old, crooked building that stood in the middle. This was called the Market Cross, and Tom knew that there was a schoolroom on the upper floor. Not that he had ever been inside it. He had never been to school, not even for a day. He couldn't read or write anything more than the three letters of his own name.

Tom was an orphan who had never known his parents. He was beaten and bullied every day. He was half-starved and owned nothing more than the rags he was wearing. And yet, despite all this, he wouldn't have described himself as unhappy. For a start he had never once been outside Framlingham, so he had nothing with which to compare his own life. At the same time he had listened to travelers staying at the inn and knew that there were poor people and hungry people all over England—so why should things be any different for him? At least he had a roof over his head, even if it was only a stable roof that leaked in the rain. He had plenty of scraps and leftovers to eat. The Slopes might beat him, but so far they hadn't broken anything. All in all, things could be worse.

Ahead of him Framlingham Castle loomed, its walls dark and ancient against the night sky. Tom had heard about the great banquets and tournaments that had taken place there years ago. But that was all in the past. Now the castle was crumbling. Cracks had appeared in the brickwork, and weeds had quickly sprouted in the cracks. The ridiculous, twisting chimneys that had been added to the battlements were just its final humiliation. Tom hurried around it, keeping the town ditch on his left. The town seemed to end very suddenly. The road became a track. The track grew more and more uneven. And then he was walking across a bumpy field with a black, skeletal forest springing up ahead.

Most of the trees had lost their leaves. The forest in winter was a cold, forbidding place. As Tom continued, branches twisted and interlocked above his head while roots formed tangled knots beneath him. The glistening tree trunks were like huge bars. With every step he took he felt himself being swallowed up by a vast, living cage. Somewhere, far away, an animal howled in the darkness. One of the dogs from the village? Or something worse? Tom knew that it was unlikely that wolves would come so far south at this time of year, but even so he found himself quickening his pace.

He had been this way many times and soon found what he was looking for. A tree shaped like a Y, a rough slope covered in white pebbles, a circular clearing, and there on the far side an old oak tree that had been hit by lightning, split in half and burned coal-black. This was the burned oak to which Sebastian Slope had referred. This was where Ratsey would be found.

Ratsey.

Tom realized that he was shivering and wondered if it was entirely due to the cold. He drew two fingers into his mouth and whistled a high-pitched note, then a lower one. It was a signal he had used often, although he still had no idea how Ratsey heard it, where he came from, or how he knew when someone was about to arrive. The sound should have echoed through the trees, but on this damp, dreary night the whistle sounded very small. Tom lifted his fingers again, then hesitated as a second terrible howl ripped through the dark sky. It *was* a wolf. It couldn't be anything else.

"Tom, Tom, the piper's son. . . ."

The voice was hushed, singing the words with a soft laugh. Tom turned around and almost cried out. A moment ago there had been no one there, but now there was a man, dressed in a long leather coat with a sword at his waist. At least, he was a man up to the neck. He had the head of some sort of horrible monster with bloodshot eyes that bulged out of their sockets, yellow teeth as thick as organ keys, swollen cheeks like overripe melons, and a chin that curved around until it almost touched his nose.

The man finished his song. "Tom, Tom, the piper's son. Will he stay or will he run?"

Tom relaxed, recognizing the voice. "Ratsey!" he exclaimed.

"Did I scare you, Tom?"

"No. . . ."

"A shame. I meant to."

Ratsey laughed, then reached up and grabbed hold of his chin. He pulled and his entire face came away—it was nothing more than an elaborate mask. The face underneath it was an unusually handsome one, with black hair sweeping over the forehead and almost touching the man's shoulders. His eyes, alight with humor, were pale blue, and the more he smiled, the brighter they seemed to shine. But for his sword, his leather coat (patched in so many places that there must have been very little of the original coat left), and his mud-spattered boots, you might have taken him for a priest or a choirboy. But then, if you had looked closer into those eyes, you might have noticed how very black his pupils were, and if at that moment he were to stop smiling, you would realize that this was a man who would never come near a church—unless it was to burn it down.

"What do you think of the new mask?" he demanded. He held it up so that its pointed nose almost touched his own.

"It's horrible," Tom replied.

"Thank you." He set the mask down. "And now, tell me, what brings you out on this wet and wicked night?"

Tom swallowed. He knew that his next words would add up to a death sentence. But he had no choice. "There is a man," he said. "A traveler."

"Is he rich?"

"Master Slope says he might be."

"Might be?" Ratsey laughed and pulled a metal bottle from somewhere inside his coat. He unscrewed the lid, raised it to his lips, and swallowed. "Tell me what *you* think, Tom-Tom! Is he rich?"

"I don't know, Ratsey."

Ratsey considered this statement for a moment. He

lowered the bottle and smacked his lips. He sighed. He sucked his teeth. And then, before Tom could move, Ratsey lashed out, grabbing hold of the boy's ear and dragging him toward him with such force that Tom cried out with pain.

"I asked you a question," he said in a reasonable tone of voice. "When I ask a question, I expect an answer. For that, my dear boy, is the point."

"He is rich!" Tom shouted. He could feel his ear coming away from his head. "He has a horse. Black, with white markings. His clothes are smart. And his purse is full."

"Which way is he coming?"

"The London road!"

"Excellent!" Ratsey let go and Tom reeled back, clutching his ear. Ratsey gazed at him apologetically, then handed him the bottle. "Here you go, my friend," he said. "Have a taste of that. Let it take away some of the cold."

Tom hesitated but Ratsey gestured, and so Tom raised the bottle to his lips. It contained some sort of brandy. The liquid burned his throat and sent tears to his eyes, but after the initial shock he felt its warmth washing through his body and he was grateful.

"You know, . . . I like you," Ratsey went on. "In a strange way, you remind me of me when I was young. Not of course that I was as scrawny and ragged as you.

As a matter of fact, my father was a duke." He winked at Tom. "Strange to think that when I was your age I ate off gold plates and had servants to do everything for me."

"So what happened, Ratsey?"

Ratsey smiled. "I got bored and I ran away. I went to war." He reached out, took the bottle back, and drank. For a long moment he gazed into the distance, and Tom could see the moon reflected in his eyes. "Captain Ratsey—that was me. I fought for the queen, in Ireland. Good old Queeny! I saw her once, you know, Tom-Tom. She was as close to me as that tree over there." He nodded at the oak. "And she turned to me. She turned to old Ratsey and she smiled. Glorious days!" Ratsey was staring at the tree, but with vague, dreamy eyes, and Tom had no doubt that he was once again seeing the queen. "But then times got hard. No money. No food. No fun. . . ." Ratsey jerked his head to one side as if shaking off the memory, and suddenly he was businesslike again. "Tell Master Slope that the trap is set," he said. "I will be a-waiting!"

"Yes, Ratsey."

The conversation was over. Tom set off at once, scrabbling across the clearing and back up the slope. When he reached the top, he stopped and turned around. But the clearing was already empty. Ratsey had vanished as quickly and quietly as he had first appeared, and the burned oak stood solitary, dead in the pale glow of the moon.

It was still dark when Tom opened his eyes the following morning. In the summer months he would be woken by the sun breaking through the cracks in the walls of the stable where he slept, but in the winter it was the cold that did it.

As he set to work, Tom thought about Ratsey and about the traveler who would be leaving for London that day. He knew what was going to happen. The same thing had been going on for as long as he could remember. But there was nothing he could do about it. It was no business of his.

Tom had just finished cleaning out the hearth—the ashes thick with fat and grease—when he became aware of voices in the main room. The first, high-pitched in anger and indignation, he knew at once. It was Sebastian Slope.

"You cannot take him!" he was saying. "I will not allow it!"

"You'll hang if you try to stop me."

A moment later the door opened and the traveler stormed in, already dressed in his cloak and with his sword buckled at his waist. Sebastian Slope was right behind him. The innkeeper had obviously gotten up in a hurry. He was wearing a dirty vest hanging outside his trousers. His eyes were bleary and his orange hair was even more disheveled than usual.

The traveler ignored him. His attention was fixed on Tom, kneeling by the hearth. "Tom," he said, "do you have any possessions? Anything you call your own?"

"No, my lord." Tom was too dazed to understand what was happening.

"Then you have nothing to pack. Come with me. We're leaving now."

"But . . . my lord!" Slope had tried bluster and that hadn't worked, so now he began to whine. "My wife and I . . . where would we be without the boy? We've treated him like a son. . . ."

"You've treated him like a slave and believe me, you will hear more on it."

"You don't want him, my lord!" Slope was actually crying but, rather repulsively, the tears were coming out what was left of his nose. "He's of no value to you. He's a sneak. He's a sniveler. If it wasn't for Mrs. S. and me, he'd have been hanged years ago."

"Tell me, boy"—the traveler was standing firmly between Tom and the innkeeper—"do you want to stay with this man and his wife?"

Tom wasn't sure what to say. He certainly had no love for either of the Slopes, but to leave . . . ? To step outside the small world of Framlingham? It was something he had never even for a minute considered.

"He wants to stay!" Slope exclaimed. "He loves Mrs. S. and me. Like we was his own parents."

"No!" Tom was amazed to find himself saying it. "I don't want to stay."

"Then we will go."

With his back turned to him, the traveler didn't see Slope snatch up a knife that had been lying on a table. Tom opened his mouth to call out a warning—but the traveler had no need of it. He must have heard something, for in less than a second his sword was out of its sheath. He spun around and slashed down twice. The first stroke gashed Slope's arm, drawing a thin line of blood. The second sliced across his stomach, and for a horrible moment Tom was sure it had killed him. But the blade had only cut through the waistband of his trousers. As Slope howled in pain, they slid down to his ankles, exposing a pair of knees like oversized walnuts.

"Follow me, Tom."

Not sure if he was awake or asleep, Tom went with the traveler into the yard and watched as he saddled and made ready his horse. It didn't take him very long. As he led the animal out of the stable, he smiled at Tom for the first time. "You have never ridden a horse," he said.

"No, my lord."

"It's not difficult. Sit behind me and hold on to me. You'll soon grow accustomed. . . ."

"Where are you taking me, my lord?"

"To London."

London!

London was a four-day ride away, but for Tom it could have been on the other side of the planet . . . on the other side of the moon even. London was a city, he knew, with a tower and a river and a cathedral so great that the church at Framlingham could fit inside it. He had heard it said that crowds of people lived there—not just dozens but hundreds, maybe even a thousand.

In silence he allowed the traveler to help him onto the horse. It was then that the door of the inn crashed open and Henrietta Slope emerged with a screech. Her husband was right behind her, half-tripping over his trousers, which he was holding up with his good hand.

"What are you doing?" she squealed. "You have no right! I'll have the law onto you!"

"I am the law," the traveler replied. "And you have every reason to fear me. But although you don't deserve it, I'll play fair with you." He threw a handful of coins into the mud. "This is for my room and board. Now be silent and let us pass."

The traveler kicked with his feet and the horse trotted forward. At the same time Henrietta threw herself in front of it. Tom wasn't sure what happened next. The horse reared up and he clung on for dear life. Henrietta fell back, losing her balance. With a great scream she crashed to the ground, slap into the middle of a pile of soft and steaming horse manure. Sebastian tried to help her, but with his trousers in a knot, he was too slow.

The horse had left the courtyard. Tom and the traveler were gone. Henrietta Slope took her husband's hand and allowed him to pull her to her feet. She gazed down the road at the horse with its two figures already vanishing into the distance. "Are you all right?" Sebastian asked.

Henrietta wiped a hand across the back of her leg. "I stink," she exclaimed.

"I know, my dear," Sebastian agreed. "But don't worry. The horse manure will hide it." He held up his hand, blood trickling between his fingers. "He cut me!" he complained.

Henrietta looked at the blood, then back at the road. "It's nothing compared to what Ratsey will do to him," she muttered.

"Ratsey!" Sebastian had forgotten, but now an ugly light came into his eyes. He tore a piece off the bottom of his vest and wrapped it around his hand. "You think he'll find him?"

"He'll find him. Ratsey never misses." Henrietta's cheeks twitched as she tried to draw lips that weren't there into a triumphant smile. "We'll have the boy back—aye, and that fine horse with him. And as for our brave traveler . . ."

"Dead meat, Mrs. S."

"Dead and buried, my beloved."

And laughing softly to themselves, the innkeeper and his wife turned and began to scavenge for the coins in the mud where they'd been thrown.

4

The Ambush

He was leaving Framlingham!

As he watched the last traces of the village disappear behind him, Tom still couldn't believe it was happening. He had been born in Framlingham. He had lived his whole life there, and he'd always assumed he would die there—probably quite soon. And not only was he leaving, he was on a horse! The Slopes could never have afforded a horse like this, even with all the money they had stolen. The only animal they'd ever owned had been a dog, and that had gone mad when they forgot to feed it.

It was the man who broke the silence.

"Tom," he said, "do you have a second name?"

"My father's name was Falconer, sir," Tom replied. "At least, that was what they put on his gravestone. But I've only ever been Tom."

"And my name is Hawkins," the traveler said.

"William Hawkins." He smiled. "A hawk and a falcon. We make a good pair."

Hawkins pulled on the reins and the horse stopped. He twisted in the saddle and gazed at the boy behind him. His eyes narrowed. He reached out and brushed the hair out of Tom's eyes. "It is most wonderful," he muttered. "You remind me of someone. I knew it the moment I first set eyes on you. But who? There's the mystery. Who indeed?"

He turned around and the horse moved off again.

"Are we really going to London, my lord?" Tom asked.

"We are."

"But why? What do you want with me?"

"It is not for me to answer your questions, Tom," Hawkins replied. "I was commanded to find you and that is what I have done. But for the rest of it . . . you'll have to wait until we arrive."

Until we arrive.

But would they?

Ever since they had set out, another fear had been stirring in Tom's mind. Gamaliel Ratsey was somewhere out there. Maybe he was even watching them now. Tom glanced around him. On one side there were fields, cut into narrow strips with rough trenches in between. On the other, trees were already beginning to thicken into a wood that would soon surround them. Hawkins had spoken of the road to London, but of course there was no real road. They were following a track that was so faint, it was barely a track at all. There was nobody else in sight.

"Why are we going this way?" Tom asked.

"This is the way I came," Hawkins replied.

"Is it the only way to London?"

"It's the fastest way. Why, Tom? What's troubling you?"

Tom wasn't sure how to answer. Part of him wanted to tell Hawkins all about Ratsey and to plead with him to go another way. But at the same time he was too afraid to speak. It was he, after all, who had warned Ratsey about the traveler only the night before—as he had done many times in the past. Tom had never been a willing part of it, but even so he knew that if Ratsey were discovered, he would hang with him.

The forest grew thicker, the silence more profound. Above them a black crow launched itself out of a tree with a sudden scream. Tom could bear it no more.

"Please, Mr. Hawkins!" he exclaimed. "You have to leave this place. You're in danger. . . ."

But it was already too late.

Ahead of them a figure suddenly stepped out, something long and metallic in its hand. The horse reared and tried to find a way around. But there were thick briars on either side. There was no other way.

Gamaliel Ratsey was wearing a mask even more hideous than the one he had worn yesterday. This one showed the head of a fish, but a fish that was already dead and rotting. Its eyes were white and sightless. Its lips were disfigured, as if torn by the fisherman's hook. Where its neck met Ratsey's shoulders, blood and green slime seemed to be oozing out.

But if the mask had been designed to frighten Hawkins, this time it hadn't worked. Quickly he brought the horse under control, then called out, "What do you want?"

"Your money!" Ratsey replied, his voice muffled behind the mask. "All of it. Your horse also. Your clothes. I like the look of your boots. And I think, while I am at it, I may also take your life!"

Hawkins said nothing. He jumped down from the horse, leaving Tom feeling very lost and alone. Ratsey glanced up, the blank fish eyes gazing at him. "Tom-Tom!" he exclaimed.

"You know the boy?" Hawkins demanded.

"Know him? Why, he and I are old friends. Drinking companions. And partners in crime."

Hawkins glanced back at Tom, uncertain for the first time. "You knew he would be here?" he asked.

"I tried to warn you," Tom answered miserably.

"Tried to warn him, Tom-Tom?" Ratsey shook his head. "Tut! Tut! Not loyal. Not nice. But enough of this idle chat. Let's kill this fellow, whoever he is, and then we can ride back together."

But Hawkins had planted his feet firmly on the ground. He threw back his cloak, revealing his sword. He turned again to Ratsey. "Whatever you may say," he said, "this boy is not with you. You and he are as different as night and day. And I warn you now to let us pass."

"Please, Ratsey!" Tom called out, though he knew it was useless. He couldn't even see Ratsey's face, but he knew that it would be as emotionless as the dead fish mask.

And he was right. "Please, Ratsey!" The highwayman echoed the words in a mocking falsetto voice.

Hawkins unsheathed his sword with a great flourish, the metal whispering against the leather scabbard.

Ratsey raised the weapon he was carrying and fired.

It was a harquebus, a type of musket. Tom had never seen such a thing before, never heard anything as loud as the explosion it made. At first he wasn't even sure what had happened. It seemed to him that Hawkins had thrown his own weapon away. Then the traveler turned, and to Tom's horror there was a great hole in the center of his chest and blood was pouring out, soaking down into his trousers, draining out of him even as Tom watched. Behind him Ratsey had lowered his gun and was muttering something, but Tom, his ears still ringing, couldn't hear him. Smoke curled up from the muzzle of the harquebus. Hawkins staggered toward him.

"To London," he rasped. "Go to Moorfield. . . ." He lifted a hand and with the last of his strength brought it down hard on the horse's rump. Tom felt the horse leap forward and he flailed out, searching for something to hold on to. Somehow his fingers found the horse's mane and he knotted them into it, his whole body tilting forward so that he seemed to be lying rather than sitting on the horse. Out of the corner of his eye he saw William Hawkins collapse, lifeless, to the ground. And there, right in front of him, was Ratsey, the fish mask already off his head and his handsome eyes staring at Tom with something like disbelief.

"Tom-Tom!" he called out.

Tom couldn't have stopped the horse even if he had wanted to. The next thing he knew, the two of them had left the ground and soared over Ratsey. Ratsey yelled and dived to one side as the horse just missed him, its back hooves grazing the side of his face. Tom was yelling too. He seemed to be flying. Then there was a great crash as the horse hit the ground again, and if Tom's hands hadn't been buried in the mane, he would have been torn loose from the saddle. Even so, the breath was punched out of him and it felt as if every bone in his body had been rattled loose. Slipping first one way, then the other, he desperately clung on as the horse thundered through the wood, swerving past the trees, leaving its dead master in the mud behind.

As the sun set that evening, three people sat around a table in The Pig's Head. None of them were speaking. They had not spoken for an hour.

Sebastian Slope was smoking a pipe that smelled of old straw. The reason for this was that it was actually filled with old straw—he had run out of tobacco. Next to him Henrietta Slope was sipping a tankard of ale, a noisy business, lacking—as she did—lips. Opposite them Gamaliel Ratsey was reading a letter by the light of a candle. He had read it several times already and taken notes, but the contents still puzzled him.

"So what does it say?" Henrietta demanded at last. "It's only two pages. It can't be that difficult."

"Actually it's in Latin," Ratsey replied. "It's also in code." He set the pages down. "The letter contains orders," he explained. "The traveler was a knight. Sir William Hawkins. A member of the Gentlemen Pensioners."

"The what?"

Ratsey sighed. "You really do know nothing about the outside world, do you," he said. "The Gentlemen Pensioners are the queen's personal bodyguards. They're closer to the queen than probably anyone else."

"What? You mean . . . ?" Sebastian had gone completely white. It looked as if he was going to be sick, and sure enough, a few moments later he was. "Do you mean the queen sent him here?" he continued when he had recovered.

"The queen or someone close to her. Yes." Ratsey nodded. "Hawkins was sent to find a boy, the son of Robert the Falconer. Somehow he knew that the boy would be at The Pig's Head . . . although that part of it isn't clear. His orders were to carry the boy to London and await further instructions. And that, of course, is where they were heading when Hawkins and I met—so unfortunately for him."

"The queen!" Sebastian was having trouble breathing. His entire face was like a slice of damp cheese. "If Hawkins was a member of the Mental Intentioners . . ."

"The Gentlemen Pensioners."

"If he was working for the queen, there'll be questions. I mean, when he doesn't arrive. They'll send constables. And worse. . . ."

"They'll hang us all," Henrietta whispered. Her fingers fluttered to her neck. "Hanged by the neck!"

"They'll probably draw and quarter us first," Ratsey remarked.

"Oh, lord!" Henrietta turned around and was as sick as her husband had been a few moments before.

"It wasn't us!" Slope exclaimed. "We didn't kill him!" He pointed the stem of his pipe at Ratsey. "It was you! You shot him in the wood!"

For the first time Ratsey's eyes grew dark. He was still smiling, but suddenly there was a chill in the room. The candle flame flickered, and black shadows slithered across his face. "Whatever happens, we should remember one thing," he said in a low voice. "We're in this together. If one of us goes down, we all do. If they plan to build a scaffold, let it be a scaffold for three."

"They can't tie us in with him," Henrietta whispered. "Hawkins came here. And he left again. What happened after that nobody knows."

"Nobody except the boy," Ratsey said.

There was a long silence.

"Young Tom saw everything," Ratsey continued after a while. "He knows all about us. And if the queen or her advisers were ever to lay their hands upon him, that could be very difficult for us."

"Where is he?" Sebastian snapped. "You had him! You let him go! This is all your fault, Ratsey."

Ratsey sighed again. He closed his eyes. Opened them. Then lashed out with his fist, catching Sebastian right on the nose. "We're all in this together," he went on. "And it seems to me that the one thing we have to do, the only thing we *can* do, is find young Tom."

"How are we going to do that?" Sebastian wailed.

Henrietta took out a filthy handkerchief and offered it to him. Both of the Slopes looked miserable and terrified.

"We know he's heading for London," Ratsey said in a reasonable tone of voice. "I'll follow him there. I'll find him and I'll kill him."

"You'll never find him in London," Sebastian gasped. He had stuffed Henrietta's handkerchief so far into his nose that only one corner of it showed. "It's a huge place. A vast place. I went there once with my father to do the Christmas shopping. It was horrible. We'd only been there a few hours and he got murdered. He didn't even have time to get me a present!"

"It is a big place," Ratsey agreed. "But I know people. And the people know people. If the boy is there, I'll hear of it soon enough." He got to his feet. "I'll see you two lovebirds in about a week," he said. "And forget about Tom. Trust me. The boy's as good as dead."

5

At the Red Lion

Three days after he had left Framlingham, Tom lost his horse, his food, and almost his life.

He had been riding hard and had stopped for the night in a small wood just outside a village. He had been too nervous to go into the village itself. He was traveling outside his parish without a license and knew that if he was caught, he would be flogged. And if they decided he was a beggar or a thief—and how else would a boy like him have his own horse?—they might burn a hole in his ear or slit his nostrils and brand him on the side of his cheek.

And so he was on his own, asleep on a bed of leaves, when the three men came. A foot breaking a branch inches from his head woke him. But he was quick-thinking enough to keep his eyes closed.

"Look at the horse!" a voice whispered.

"It's a beauty!" whispered the second.

"Take it! Take it! And cut the boy's throat!" That was a third voice, slithering out of the night.

"No need to kill him," the first voice replied. "He's asleep. . . ."

"Then take the horse."

"I have it."

"Quick."

And then they were gone.

Tom sat up, shivering. It had been a close escape. If he had so much as opened his eyes, a knife would have been the last thing he would have seen.

It was harder after that. For two whole days he walked. The rain never stopped, and soon he felt as if the water were going right through him. He had no food. After twenty-four hours his head was spinning and he could barely see the road ahead. At the start of his journey he had done his best to avoid people. Now it was the other travelers who avoided him. He was a doomed, half-frozen boy, dying on his feet. Nobody wanted to come near.

On the sixth day, just after the sun had set, Tom came to a town. At least, he assumed it must be a town. He had never seen so many tall and solid buildings so close together.

The first of these was an inn. It was three floors high, its windows ablaze with light, with flaming torches in front of the main door. The front of the inn was a brilliant pattern of black beams and white panels, with a wooden balcony running all the way along the front. A cobbled pathway led underneath a wide arch and into an inner courtyard, and even as Tom watched, a great carriage pulled by four horses arrived and rattled past, under, and in. Immediately two hostlers dressed in brown aprons appeared and ran forward to help the passengers dismount. At the same time a huge man with a black beard appeared, laughing at nothing in particular and chewing what looked like a leg of lamb. Somehow Tom knew that this was the landlord.

"Welcome, welcome!" the man bellowed. "All men are welcome at the Red Lion of Enfield. Come in! Come in!"

Tom watched as they went in, laughing and chattering among themselves. For a moment he swayed on his feet. He had no more strength left. If this was London, then London would be where he would die. He took a deep breath. His position was hopeless. He had nothing to lose. With the last of his strength he forced himself across the road. The innkeeper had just seen the last of the guests into the building when he noticed Tom, covered in mud from head to foot and looking more like a broken-down scarecrow than a thirteen-year-old boy.

The innkeeper frowned. "What do you want?" he demanded.

"Please, sir"—Tom had to concentrate to make his lips move—"may I work for you?"

"Work for me? What the devil makes you think I need a young beggar like you? What work do you want? What work can you do?"

"I can tend to the horses, sir. I worked at an inn. In Framlingham. . . ."

"Framlingham?" The innkeeper's eyes narrowed. "That's many miles from here. Run away, have you? Do you know what happens to the cursed cheats who run away from their masters?"

Tom was too tired to argue. He turned around and was about to leave when the innkeeper grabbed hold of him and yelled out, "Quickly!"

The door opened and a plump, gray-haired woman dressed in an apron and cap came out. She had a narrow face with a pointed chin and such wide eyes that she seemed to be permanently amazed about everything. "Yes?" she demanded.

"See for yourself, Mistress Quickly," the innkeeper replied. "This young apple-squire is demanding work. Would you believe it?"

Quickly—for it seemed that was her name—glanced at Tom with distaste. "He's more mud than boy," she remarked. "In fact, he's a muddy disgrace!"

"Exactly what I thought you would say!" the innkeeper boomed. "So what shall we do with him?"

"Well, let's take him inside. I mean, look at him! He's standing in a piddle." She pulled Tom out of a puddle. "I think I have a perfect task for him!"

"Good for you, Mistress Quickly," the landlord cried. "You be sure that our little gypsy works. Hard work. Nonstop work. That is the order of the day!"

Tom allowed himself to be dragged into the Red Lion, his head spinning. He had never been inside a building quite like it. Pewter plates piled high with food being carried to tables flashed in front of his eyes. There were pigeons and pastries, eggs and oysters, lamb, beef, pork, and huge, golden chickens. Hundreds of candles burned in the inn, but they were hardly needed with the glow of not one but three fires, turning everything bright red. And the people! Tom had never seen so many people dressed in the finest clothes, talking and laughing as they ate.

"Through here!"

Tom found himself being pushed through a door, and suddenly he was in the kitchen—where, of course, he belonged. But, with a heavy heart, Tom knew that he couldn't work. He could barely stand. And when the woman saw he was good for nothing, he would soon be back out in the rain.

"Very well," Mistress Quickly exclaimed. "I want you to sit here, child." She gestured at a seat next to a fire. "Your task is to make sure that the fire doesn't go out. Do you understand?"

"Yes." Tom nodded. "I'm to watch the fire."

"You are also to taste *all* the food you are given. I need to know that it's malicious. I'll ask you to taste a little wine as well, I think. For the same reason. Do you think you can manage all that? Sitting by the fire? Eating and drinking?"

Tom nodded, amazed.

"Good, good, good!" Mistress Quickly beamed. "I'll snatch up with you later." And then she was gone.

Tom couldn't believe his good fortune. He knew of course that these weren't really jobs at all, that the innkeeper and the woman had taken pity on him and had saved him from death by cold and starvation. It was the first time anyone had been kind to him in his entire life, and a short while later when a smiling girl brought him a plate of meat and bread and a cup of wine, he had to fight to keep the tears from his eyes. After that he slept, half-leaning against the wall, the flames from the fire warming his hands and face.

When he awoke, someone was towering over him. He looked up, alarmed, but it was only Mistress Quickly.

"Recovered your strength?" she asked.

"Yes. Thank you. . . ."

"Child! There's no need to spank me!" She smiled. "Have you ever seen a play?"

"No," Tom said.

"Then you're fortunate. We have the players in tonight. Come out and see."

The only entertainment Tom had ever seen in Framlingham had been minstrels (usually out-of-tune) and jugglers. A bear-baiter had once visited the town with an old, half-starved bear. But the sight of the poor animal being stoned and tormented had only made him feel miserable. Another time a group of players had stayed at The Pig's Head, but they hadn't performed—the parish didn't approve of plays. The fact was that Tom had very little idea what a play even was. He doubted he would be able to understand it and thought it would be rather dull.

But when he followed Mistress Quickly into the courtyard, the first thing he heard was roars of laughter from the crowd, who now lined the balconies leading around the inside of the inn and who were packed neck-and-neck on the ground below. The players—about a dozen of them—had set themselves up at the far end, using one wall of the inn as the backdrop to a makeshift stage. Torches and candles blazed everywhere, turning night into day. And as Tom watched, they acted out their story, turning the Red Lion into another world.

It was a mad story.

The play was about two sets of identical twins—two masters and two servants—who accidentally turned up in the same city. Because they looked exactly the same, the masters kept on confusing the twins and the twins kept on mistaking the masters until everyone was chasing everyone else all around the stage. Tom soon found himself swept up in a way he had never known before. It was as if all his own problems were forgotten. For two hours William Hawkins, the Slopes, and Gamaliel Ratsey simply didn't exist. It was a wonderful feeling, to be so lost in something that nothing else mattered.

If Tom had kept his eyes on the stage like everyone else, he might not have seen what happened next. But he enjoyed watching the audience too—he had never seen so many people having such a good time—and it was while his eyes were on them that he saw the thief at work.

The thief was a boy a couple of years older than himself. He was wearing a thick red cloak with a tall hat on his head and brown trousers ballooning out at the knees. The boy had a rather round face, long, fair hair, and thick lips.

The boy was standing right behind a wealthy-looking merchant, and as Tom watched, he reached forward, his hand disappearing underneath the man's cloak. At the same time his other hand drew out a short sword and cut through the man's purse. Tom gasped. It had taken less than five seconds, and now the purse was in the boy's pocket and he was already moving on to the next person in the crowd.

Mistress Quickly was standing next to Tom. "What is it?" she demanded.

"There! He stole that man's purse!" Tom lifted his hand and pointed at the boy. At that very moment the boy looked up at Tom. And to Tom's astonishment his face broke into a broad smile.

But Mistress Quickly wasn't amused. "A foist!" she yelled. "There's a pockpicket in the house!"

At once the play was forgotten as the audience exploded. They knew there was a thief among them. The only trouble was, they didn't know who he was.

"There!" Mistress Quickly shouted again.

The thief took one last glance at Tom. Slowly he shook his head as if to reproach Tom for spoiling his fun. Then he pointed at a fat, bald man two rows behind him. "That's him!" the thief cried out.

"What . . . ?" the bald man began, then yelled as someone punched him full on the nose. The bald man reeled back, blood flying, then crashed into two more members of the audience. This sparked off a second fight, and moments later the entire audience was shouting and swearing, exchanging blows, and sprawling over the courtyard. On the stage the actors tried to continue the scene, realized it was hopeless, and stopped to watch. Now it was the actors who had become the audience and the audience who provided the entertainment. Just in front of the stage two men began a sword fight. A very old lady lashed out with a surprisingly strong fist. A merchant had the shirt ripped off his shoulders, while two more grappled with each other's beards.

Tom looked down at the battlefield, searching for the boy who had started it all. A moment later he saw him. The boy had reached the archway and was slipping out into the street. The boy looked back and saw Tom. He took out his stolen purse and raised it in a defiant gesture, then drew a quick finger across his nose. His meaning was clear: To hell with you! To hell with you all!

Then the boy turned, and a moment later he had gone.

6

Paul's Walk

The following morning Mistress Quickly and the innkeeper said their good-byes. There was a cart making the short journey from Enfield to London, and they had arranged for Tom to be given a ride.

"You look after yourself, young rakehell!" the innkeeper boomed. "And when you reach London, be sure you head for St. Paul's."

"Where is that?" Tom asked.

"St. Paul's Cathedral. You can't miss it. Ask for Paul's Walk. That's the best place to find honest work."

"Farewell!" Mistress Quickly cried. "It was lovely beating you!"

The cart set off, and although Tom had slept well the night before, he found his eyes closing once again. Soon he had drifted back into sleep.

He was woken by the sound of a bell tolling. He sat up and blinked. The cart was rumbling past a priory with a cluster of neat houses lying in its shadow, and at first Tom thought he was still in the countryside. Behind him there were fields and gently sloping hills. But when he twisted around and looked ahead, more and more houses and shops sprang up, and a moment later he knew that they had plunged into the city itself.

London!

It was the noise that struck him first. There were people everywhere, shouting and shoving as they tried to reach the market stalls. At the same time, the stall-owners and shopkeepers were shouting back at them, all of them trying to make themselves heard. "What do you lack? What do you lack?"—this from the shopkeepers, standing in their doorways—"Sweep! Chimney sweep!" "Ripe apples red!" "Fine Seville Oranges!"—at every street corner there was someone with something to sell. Horses stamped and stumbled in the mud. Cartwheels creaked and rattled. Dogs barked and cows bellowed their protests as they were driven to market. In work-shops open to the street, half-naked metalworkers smashed down with their hammers and yelled instructions to their hurrying apprentices. Carpenters in leather aprons sawed and chiseled. A group of sailors wove past, half-drunk already, singing and laughing. So much noise! Tom pressed his hands to his ears and tried to stop his head from spinning.

And then there were the smells. Vegetables and

spices in the market. Fruit—fresh and rotting. Great hunks of cheese. Kegs of rich ruby wine. The smell of people, sweating and dirty. The smell of animals. And of course, the worst smell of all, coming from an open drain that ran down the center of the road, a foul-colored stream that never stopped flowing, carrying all the sewage of London to who could say where!

Tom climbed out of the cart, marveling at all the people around him. Colorful signs hung in the air, advertising the shops below. A black horse, a white rose, a yellow snake. Higher up, the inhabitants had stretched lines from one side of the street to the other so that they could hang out their clothes, which fluttered like misshapen flags against the blue sky. A woman in expensive dress hurried past, pressing a scentbottle to her nose and trying not to look at anything. In the distance a group of boys were throwing mud-balls and laughing at a man with dark skin and foreign-looking clothes—presumably a visitor.

"Dirty postcard?" A man with a broken nose, several broken teeth, and a badly twisted neck had suddenly stepped in front of Tom. "Do you want to buy a dirty postcard?" he asked.

"No. . . ."

"Each one's engraved! And you won't find a filthier sonnet!"

"No, thank you."

The innkeeper had advised Tom to go to St. Paul's Cathedral and that at least was easy to find. The driver of the cart pointed the way, and Tom followed a narrow, curving lane until it suddenly opened into a great square where a priest, dressed in black and white, was addressing a crowd of a hundred people. The cathedral stood behind them, a mountain of brick and stone, of soaring windows and towers. Tom wouldn't have believed it was possible to build anything as big as this. The main tower seemed almost to touch the sky—and surely would have if only it hadn't managed to lose its steeple.

He went inside.

It was almost lunchtime and St. Paul's was beginning to empty. Tom walked slowly up the center aisle, its great stone pillars standing like some enchanted forest all around him. A door slammed shut and the sound echoed through the chamber. There were a few men lounging against the pillars. Some were talking in low voices. In the shadows, one man was counting coins into the outstretched palm of another. Everyone in the church seemed to be watching someone else, and it occurred to Tom that nobody was actually praying.

He reached a tall wooden door covered from top to bottom with slips of paper. A handful of men had been examining these as Tom approached, but now the men dispersed and he found himself alone. The pieces of paper were covered with words. Tom recognized a few of the letters, but of course he couldn't read.

"What are you looking for, my dear boy?"

The speaker was a small, fat man, almost as round as he was tall. He reminded Tom of a snowman. His eyes were as black as coal. His nose was long and pointed. And his head seemed to balance on his shoulders without the benefit of a neck. He was wearing black trousers and a white shirt, frayed at the elbows. The fur on his collar looked suspiciously like rat.

"What?" Tom wasn't even sure that the man was talking to him.

"You're new in the town." The man smiled. His lips were wet and rubbery. "I have not, I think, seen you here before."

"I arrived today." Tom was afraid to give any information away. He had taken an immediate dislike to the man without quite knowing why.

But the man seemed unaware of it. "You have come to the right place," he said. "My name is Grimly. James Grimly at your service!" He tried to bow, but his stomach was too round and didn't have anywhere to bend. "So you are searching for employment?"

"I might be. . . ."

"How nice." The man ran his eyes over Tom as if he

were inspecting a horse or a piece of meat. "If you were—that is—searching for work," he went on, "I might be able to help."

"How?"

"I have a large number of people in my employ. Young lads like yourself. James Grimly's boys are well-known on the streets of London."

"What sort of work do they do?" Tom asked, feeling more uneasy by the minute.

"Charity work," Grimly explained. He giggled. "Yes. There are people, you see, who need to give to charity. And so it follows that there must be people who *are* charity. That is what I supply. That, if you like, is my boys."

Tom didn't quite understand this, but knew he did not like it. "Thank you, Mr. Grimly," he said, "but no."

"Your choice, my dear fellow. Of course it is! Maybe soon you'll think again. But for now I leave you to dine with Duke Humphrey!"

Tom frowned, not knowing what he meant.

Grimly pointed at a large stone tomb. "Humphrey, Duke of Gloucester!" he explained. "No money? No food? Then you are on your own with him!" The little man laughed and walked away, his boots clattering on the stone floor.

Relieved to see him go, Tom turned and was about to go back the way he had come, when he stopped and froze.

The main door must have opened and closed while he was talking to Grimly. A man had come in and was talking to another cluster of men, asking them questions. Even from a distance, Tom recognized his long black hair, his slim, languid body, his penetrating blue eyes. Gamaliel Ratsey had followed him to London. Somehow he had overtaken him on the road. If he so much as raised his head, he would see Tom. Tom knew he had to hide.

He looked the other way. James Grimly had almost reached the far door, and before he knew quite what he was doing, Tom had caught up with him. Grimly's snowball head swiveled on his shoulders. He didn't look surprised to see Tom.

"My dear boy!" he said. "My most likeable fellow! Do I take it that you have already reconsidered?"

"Yes," Tom blurted out. "I have." He was almost whispering, afraid that Ratsey would hear him even though he was all the way on the other side of the cathedral.

"Then let us hurry to my offices before you change your mind again," Grimly said. "We must prepare you for your work. It will mean certain . . . changes. The sooner they're done, the sooner you can start."

Tom nodded, although he had heard little of what the man had said.

Leaving Paul's Walk behind them, the two set off together.

Grimly had a yard at the end of a dark, narrow alleyway near the Thames. The city was much quieter here, with fewer people on the streets and a damp, evil-smelling fog in the air. Slimy water and mud rose over Tom's ankles as the two of them hurried toward a pair of moldering wooden gates.

"My home," Grimly muttered. He opened the gates and ushered Tom inside.

The gates led into a rough, partly cobbled courtyard, squeezed between three buildings that seemed to be leaning on each other to stay upright. Tom looked around him, growing more uneasy by the minute. Set in the middle of the courtyard was a single wooden chair with a high back and solid arms and legs. Tom had no idea what the chair was for. But there was something about it that made him go cold inside.

"Belter!" Grimly called. "Snivel! Fetch the book! Show yourselves! We have a new recruit!"

Almost at once a door at the side of the courtyard flew open and two men hurried out. The first of these, the man called Belter, was huge, muscular, and completely bald with a face that hadn't quite formed, like an

oversized baby. He was naked to the waist. He had no
hair on his chest and his nipples were black. Snivel was
older, a crumpled bag of a man, carrying a leather-bound
book underneath his withered arm.

"A new recruit?" Snivel rasped. He licked his lip.
"From Paul's Walk?" he asked.

"Where else?" Grimly turned to Tom. "We will prepare you straightaway."

"Prepare me?" Tom was getting more nervous by the
second. "What do you mean?"

"I thought I told you. We must prepare you for charity!"

"Charity!" Snivel agreed.

"What sort of charity?" Tom demanded.

Grimly sighed. "The homeless and the disabled," he
explained. "I have boys all over London. On street cor-
ners. Outside churches. They are Grimly's boys."

"You mean they're beggars!"

"Indeed so. But special beggars. They are employed
by me and I take half of what they earn. But in return I
help them, you see. I *adjust* them." Grimly flicked a finger in Tom's direction. "Consider a boy like yourself. A
little thin. A little ragged. Yes. But what do you think
that's worth? Good people, charitable people, people
with money . . . they want something more. Oh, yes, they
might give a penny to a child shivering with cold. But

how much more do you think they would give to that same child, *missing a leg?*"

Grimly had barely spoken the last three words before Tom was running for the gate. But Belter had been expecting it. Before Tom had taken two paces he was grabbed from behind and dragged, screaming, to the wooden chair. There was nothing he could do as he was forced down, his hands and feet securely fastened with rope. It was over in a matter of seconds. By the time the giant had finished with him, Tom was sitting helplessly, unable to move.

"Let me go!" he shouted. "I've changed my mind! I don't want to work for you!"

Grimly touched a finger to his lips. "Don't shout," he said in a soft, soothing voice. "It will hurt only for a short time."

Belter had produced a dirty canvas bag from somewhere. He dropped it on the cobbled floor and Tom heard it clink.

"Now what shall we do with him?" Grimly asked. "How about one arm and one leg?"

Snivel had opened his book. "We did one of those last week," he said.

"All right then. Just the legs." Grimly smiled at Tom. "He's a handsome fellow. Interesting hair color. Nice eyes. Let's leave the top half alone."

Belter grabbed hold of him and Tom screamed.

Then the doors of the yard crashed open.

Tom was too far gone to understand fully what was happening, but he became dimly aware that Belter had straightened up again and that Grimly was walking forward with a look of annoyance on his face. "You!" he exclaimed. "What are you doing here?"

Tom forced his head to turn so that he could see the new arrival. A boy a few years older than himself was standing by the open door, leaning against the wall and smoking a pipe. He was looking at the scene with what could only be described as an amused smile. Tom thought he had seen the boy somewhere before, but he told himself that was impossible.

"Let the boy go," the new arrival demanded.

"What?" Grimly looked more sad than angry. "But he came here of his own choice," he protested. "I found him at Paul's Walk. . . ."

"Oh, yes! And you explained to him all about your little 'adjustments,' I'm sure. Just like all the others!"

"Wait a minute! Wait a minute! We can talk about this . . . !"

Out of the corner of his eye Tom saw Snivel reaching into a fold in his shirt. While Grimly prattled on, the old man's hand inched out and now it was holding a wicked-looking knife. Tom opened his mouth to call out a warning to the boy, but there was no need. In a single movement he swept back his cloak to reveal a short sword, which was suddenly out of its scabbard and in his hand, slicing through the air. The blade caught the edge of the knife, tore it out of Snivel's hand, and sent it spinning through the air to clatter harmlessly on the ground. Then the point of the boy's sword was at Grimly's throat, pressing against the skin.

"Please!" Grimly's black eyes bulged. A bead of sweat trickled over his neck. "This is just business. It has nothing to do with you. He's my boy. I found him."

The older boy shook his head and pressed a little harder with the sword. "Not this one, Grimly. He's a friend of mine. Let him go."

A friend of mine? So Tom was right. He had seen the boy somewhere before. But where?

Grimly had one last try. "But look at him!" he moaned. "Nice face. Intelligent eyes. But sad with it. We were just going to take off his legs. He'll make us a fortune."

"Maybe," the boy replied. "But you won't be alive to enjoy it." His hand tightened on the sword. "You tried to recruit me when I first arrived in the city," he went on. "And I often think I should have cut your throat then. London would be better off without you, Grimly. And all I need is another excuse. . . ."

"No! Take him!" Grimly was on the edge of tears, and his voice was a whisper. Belter and Snivel ran forward, and a few seconds later the ropes had fallen away and Tom was able to stand up.

"Come this way," the boy said. He had lowered his sword, but his eyes never left the three men.

Tom staggered over to him, and he and the boy left the yard. It was only when they had reached the end of the alley and emerged into the main street that he realized two things.

The first thing was that he did know the boy. He had seen him the night before at the Red Lion, stealing a purse in the middle of the play.

And the second thing was that he wasn't a boy at all. He might be wearing trousers, carrying a sword, and smoking a pipe. But Tom had just been rescued by a girl!

7

Moll Cutpurse

My name," she said, "is Moll Cutpurse."

"Cutpurse?" Tom frowned. "Is that your real name?"

"One of them. I have many." Moll thought for a moment. "I used to be called Mary, but I soon put an end to that. Much too girlish." She rubbed her chin as if hoping to find stubble there. "You would not wish to be a girl," she said. "Not in the sixteenth century!"

"What do you do?" Tom asked.

"What do you think I do?" Moll exclaimed. "I'm a thief. A very qualified thief. In fact, I came in first in my class!"

She and Tom were sitting in a small, square room above a shoe shop. The building was perched on the south bank of the river, so close that Tom could hear the water lapping against the brickwork. The single room contained a bed, two chairs, a table, a cupboard, and a small fire that struggled to keep out the damp. However, the windows had glass. The roof didn't leak. And, as Moll was quick to point out, it didn't have rats.

She had warmed up some stew over the fire and served it on two thick slices of bread—she had no plates. Somewhere she had found a bottle of wine. Now the two of them were gazing at each other over the table.

"I daresay you want to know how I found you," Moll said.

"Yes."

"It was luck, really. I was at St. Paul's Walk. I go there, as does everyone. I saw you meet up with Grimly and I followed you."

"But why? Why did you save me?"

"Because I wanted to kill you myself."

Tom stared. Moll was still wearing her sword and he waited for her to draw it—but her hands didn't move.

"You cost me a small fortune at the Red Lion," she went on. "Never had I seen so many purses, and I'd have had a dozen of them if it hadn't been for you. And you could have got me hanged!"

"I'm sorry."

"It's a bit late for that now."

Tom gestured at the sword. "So why haven't you?" he asked. "Killed me, I mean."

Moll shrugged. "Because if you were stupid enough

to go off with James Grimly, you were probably too stupid to know what you were doing at the Red Lion. Anyway, don't ask too many questions or I may change my mind."

Moll got up and put another piece of wood on the fire. Tom looked around. There were only the two of them in the room, but he couldn't shake off the feeling that they were being watched. He turned to the window. It was growing dark and there were no boats out on the Thames.

"Do you have parents?" he asked.

"My father used to run the shoe shop downstairs," Moll replied. "But he died of the plague. My mother too. I think I had a brother, but he disappeared. Anyway, I'm on my own now."

There was a long silence. Moll leaned forward and put another log on the fire. The flames reached out tiredly to consume it.

"Can I stay here?"

"You're not serious!"

"I have nowhere else to go."

"That's your problem." Moll glanced at Tom and sighed. "All right. One night. Maybe two. But I have no liking for boys. Particularly stupid boys who don't know what they're doing. What *are* you doing? I suppose you're a runaway. Left your master, have you?"

"I didn't run away. It wasn't like that."

"Then what was it like? You might as well tell me. Not that I'm offering to help. . . ."

So Tom told her his story: his life with the Slopes and Gamaliel Ratsey, the arrival of William Hawkins, and the ambush in the woods. Moll's eyes narrowed when she heard Ratsey's name, and when Tom told her how he had seen Ratsey at Paul's Walk, she shook her head doubtfully. "You know him?" Tom asked her.

"I have heard of him. Everyone has heard of Ratsey. But it's unlike him to be down here in London. And I think it's bad news for you."

"That's what I thought," Tom agreed.

"He's dangerous. As long as he's here, you're in danger. He'll find you soon enough. And when he does, well . . . " Moll drew a finger across her throat.

"That's very encouraging," Tom muttered.

Moll thought for a moment. "Tell me more about Hawkins," she said.

"I've told you everything I know."

"That's the part of your story that makes no sense." Moll took out her pipe and lit it. "He was obviously a gentleman. Maybe even a member of the court. He asks questions about you and about your parents, and then he seizes you and brings you back here. . . ."

"He said I should go to Moorfield," Tom said.

"But why? What did he want with you? A nobody. A

nothing. A stable boy who barely knows one end of a horse from the other."

"Thank you!"

"And why Moorfield?" Moll sighed and blew out a perfect smoke ring. "I suppose I could take you there."

"You know where it is?"

"Of course I do. It's just outside the City Wall. We could walk there in half an hour. But I wouldn't get too excited. There's nothing there. A few butts. Some windmills. If that's what he brought you all this way to see, he was wasting your time."

"Maybe he lived there."

"Nobody smart lives in Moorfield. How do you think it got its name? It used to be a moor. Now it's a field."

"At least we can look," Tom said gloomily.

Moll nodded. "All right. So we shall. But it's too late in the day to go there now. The sun will be down in an hour or so. We'll go there tomorrow morning."

"What about tonight?" Tom looked around the room. "You said I could stay here?"

"Yes."

"But there's only one bed."

"That's right. You can have the floor."

From the moment he had walked into Moll's room, Tom had felt that he was being watched. But it was only later that night, as he lay on the floor with a single blanket and the flickering fire to keep him warm, that he realized by whom. The room looked out not just on the river, but about fifty yards upstream, on London Bridge. The huge bridge with its twenty stone arches and its shops, houses, and chapels all crammed together above the water was one of the great sights of the city. But it was only now, as he gazed at it in the moonlight, that Tom noticed something else. There *were* three heads turned toward the window, three pairs of eyes fixed on him even now. But they were eyes that saw nothing. The heads they belonged to ended at the neck, cut off and stuck on metal poles.

Traitors. This was the price they had paid.

Tom rolled over and pulled the blanket over his head. But he could still feel the eyes boring into him. And it was a long, long time before he lost himself in the brief escape of sleep.

Moll was right about Moorfield.

She and Tom were standing in a rectangular field just north of the City Wall. Far away to the north Tom could just make out the shape of three windmills. There were a few cows grazing here and there. Despite the icy weather—it seemed to be getting colder by the day—a handful of people had come out to practice archery, aiming at two straw-filled targets, the "butts" that Moll had mentioned. It was a sunny day, but the sun was white, not yellow, and gave no warmth at all. Somewhere dogs were barking. Otherwise Moorfield was empty and silent.

"Seen enough?" Moll asked.

"Yes."

"Maybe you didn't hear him properly. Maybe he didn't want to bring you here."

"He definitely said Moorfield."

Moll shrugged. "Let's drink something," she said. "I'm chilled to the bone!"

They turned south and went through Moorgate, back into the city. That was the strange thing about London. It was huge, crowded, the streets and houses jammed into what little space there was between the wall and the river. But walk ten minutes in almost any direction and suddenly you had left it all behind you and were back in the countryside. It was a city surrounded by green.

Moll led Tom into a tavern, took the table nearest the fire, and ordered two pints of ale. Neither of them spoke until it came. At last Moll lit her pipe and broke the silence. "So what are you intending to do now?" she asked.

Tom was feeling more miserable than ever. In all the time he had been traveling from Framlingham, and despite what Moll had said the night before, he had been hoping that Moorfield would mean something, be something. That when he got there, everything would make sense. But a field, a handful of cows, and three wind-mills? Why should Hawkins have brought him all the way from Framlingham for that? "I don't know," he said.

"Maybe you should leave London. If you have Ratsey looking for you . . ."

"But where will I go?" Tom cried. "I have nowhere."

"I'm told Bristol's nice. You could join the navy."

"I'd get seasick," Tom said.

"How about the army?"

"That's worse. I'd get shot."

Moll slammed down her tankard. "I knew it was a mistake coming after you," she muttered. "Now I'm stuck with you. A boy! The last thing I need!"

"Maybe I could learn how to be a thief . . . like you?" Tom suggested. But even as he spoke the words, he knew it wouldn't work. Tom lived in a world where there were as many thieves as honest men. He had spent his entire life surrounded by them. He knew that many people had a simple choice: Steal or starve. But even so, there was something inside him that told him that steal-ing was wrong and that it wouldn't work for him. His heart would never be in it.

Moll must have sensed this because she shook her head. "No. You're not a thief."

"Then what?"

"Listen to me." Moll leaned forward. "If you are

going to stay in London, you must go somewhere Ratsey won't find you. And that means you can't stay with me, even if I wanted you to, which I don't. Everyone knows everyone down here. Paul's Walk isn't just a meeting place. It's where everyone finds out about everyone else. That's why he was there yesterday, and that's why he'll be there today." Moll looked nervously over her shoulder. "We've been in here thirty minutes," she went on, "and who knows who may have seen us together? Someone could be on their way to Ratsey even now. You stay with me, he'll find you soon enough. Believe me. You won't be safe with me."

Tom nodded, feeling gloomier by the minute.

"We have to find you work. You need money in your pocket and a roof over your head."

"But what sort of work can I do?" Tom sighed.

"That's a good question." Moll thought for a minute. "I could find you a place in a tavern. You say you've handled horses, and there are people I know. No"—she shook her head—"forget it. Ratsey knows your past and that's the first place he'll look. He's probably searching every tavern in town even as we sit."

"What else?"

Moll thought for a moment, toying with her pipe. "Can you cook?" she asked.

"No."

"Can you read?"

"No."

"Can you sew?"

"No."

"Can you sing?"

"I've never tried."

Moll sighed. "A typical boy. Completely useless. All right. There's nothing you *can* do. But is there anything you *want* to do? At least that might be worth a try."

Tom thought hard. What did he want to do? Here he was in London, the greatest city in the world. He could be anything he wanted to be. But what *did* he want to be? Not a thief. Not a beggar. Could he work in the market? No. He would never make himself heard in all that din. How about a shop assistant? No. That would mean handling money and he couldn't count.

And then he remembered. He had only ever been completely happy once in all his thirteen years. For just a few brief hours all his problems had been forgotten, and it was as if he had been transported to another world. At that moment Tom knew that there was only one thing he wanted to be. He wanted to join the people he had seen two nights before, at the Red Lion of Enfield.

"I know what I want to do, Moll," he said. "I want to join the theatre. I want to act."

8

Auditions

I still think it's a foolish idea," Moll said.

"But you don't like the theatre," Tom replied.

"I love the theatre! I go there all the time."

"Yes. But only to rob the audiences."

It was six o'clock in the morning, two days after their unsuccessful visit to Moorfield. Tom was still lying on the floor, wrapped in a blanket, but Moll was already up and fully dressed—which was hardly surprising, as she slept in her clothes. The day before, she had visited Paul's Walk and come back with exciting news. An advertisement had been posted on the Si Quis door (this was the name of the door that Tom had himself noticed). Actors were wanted for a new play that was about to be performed at the Rose Theatre, not far from where Moll lived. Those interested were to present themselves at the theatre, where auditions would be taking place.

And now it was the day of the auditions. Tom had barely slept a wink the night before. It was a strange thing. He had never once in his entire life thought about becoming an actor. But now that he had made the decision, there was nothing he wanted more. It was as if it had been in his blood all along, but had only now bubbled to the surface.

Moll was holding a package wrapped in paper. "This is for you."

Tom threw the blanket off and sat up. "What is it?" he asked.

Moll was suddenly uncomfortable. "Don't you even know what it is in four days' time?" she snapped. "It's Christmas Day. So this is your present."

"You went and bought me a present?" Tom was amazed. Nobody had ever bought him anything. Then a nasty thought crossed his mind. "Did you really *buy* it?" he asked.

"I didn't steal it, if that's what you mean. I used my own money."

"But you stole the money. . . ."

"Well . . . yes."

Tom unwrapped the package. Inside was a white shirt, a pair of woolen trousers, a waistcoat, and most wonderful of all, a pair of leather boots. Tom held them, marveling. He had been barefoot for as long as he could remember. This leather, soft and warm in his hands, was something he had only ever dreamed about. He gazed at her, unbelieving.

"Thank you, Moll," he said.

"Don't thank me," Moll replied. "I only did it to be rid of you. I mean, you'll never get a job as an actor if you turn up looking like a beggar. Now get dressed. We ought to be on our way."

They left a few minutes later, Tom wearing his new clothes. Taking off his old clothes had been like shedding his own skin. He had worn the same shirt and trousers for about three years, and they had stayed on him day and night. To walk without feeling the mud or being cut by jagged stones was a completely new experience for him, and he had tripped three times before he had even left the house. As he walked down the street, he wondered how he must look to other people. The clothes Moll had bought weren't new, but they were clean. He felt almost like a gentleman.

The Rose Theatre was a large round building, part wood, part plaster, and part brick. It stood in what had once been a garden—that was how it got its name. It was still early in the morning, but already a lot of actors had come to audition—men in feathered caps and flowing cloaks, preening themselves like pigeons.

Moll stopped opposite the main door. "Well. Good luck to you," she said.

"Are you not coming in?" Tom asked.

"No." She shook her head. "There's always a chance I might be recognized. I spent a busy night here last month." She took Tom's hand. "You know where to find me if you need me. But I'm sure they'll take you on. You look like an actor. You have an actor's eyes."

"Thanks, Moll."

"If they do hire you, come back and see me on Christmas Day. I'm going out for the midday meal. A reunion. You might enjoy it."

"I'm sure I'll be back tonight," Tom said.

"I hope not," Moll retorted. "My room's only big enough for one. And your feet smell."

Moll turned and walked away. Tom watched her until she'd gone. Then, taking a deep breath, he crossed the road and went into the Rose.

He found himself in a circular space with seats rising in three tiers and surrounding him on all sides. In front of him was a raised stage with two pillars holding up a slanting tiled roof. There were two doors at the back, presumably where the actors made their entrances. The theatre had no roof. If it rained (or snowed—the weather was getting colder and colder), the actors and the audience in front of the stage would get soaked. Only the people in the seats would have any chance of staying dry.

There was an actor standing in the middle of the stage, reciting what sounded like a poem in a whiny and monotonous voice. Two more men were watching him, sitting on stools to one side. They were both expensively dressed. Both of them looked bored.

The actor had recited only about three lines when one of the men stood up. "That's enough, thank you," he called out. "Next!"

"But I've only just begun!" the actor whined.

"Don't send a messenger to us. We'll send a messenger to you," the man replied.

The actor left the stage. There was a long line of men snaking around the edge of the theatre. As soon as he had gone, one of them took his place and the line moved forward. Tom walked toward the stage, thrilled and terrified by it at the same time. Could he stand here and perform—perhaps for a hundred or two hundred people? He wanted to. He was being drawn to the stage like a fish on a hook. He felt he belonged there. He felt . . .

"Look out!"

With his eyes fixed on the stage, Tom had collided with a young man who had been carrying a sheaf of papers. Now the papers fell out of his hands and cascaded to the floor, some of them carried by the breeze into the very muddiest of puddles. Every page was covered with writing, and Tom was horrified to see the words blur and then disappear in a black haze as they came into contact with the water.

"I'm sorry! I'm really sorry. . . ."

Tom did his best to scoop the pages out of the puddle and hand them back to the man.

"Why couldn't you look where you were going?"

"I was looking at the stage. I'm sorry." Tom straightened up, feeling wretched. Here he was in his brand-new clothes and already he had made a complete idiot of himself.

The man glanced at him and softened. "It wasn't your fault," he said. "I wasn't looking either. I was thinking about my new play."

Tom looked at the man more carefully. He was in his late twenties, dressed in a black velvet tunic with a high white collar. The man had an unusually intelligent face. His deep brown eyes seemed to look right into you, through you, and at you at the same time. His hair, also brown, hung almost down to his neck at the back and sides, but he was already going bald on top.

"A new play?" Tom realized what the man had just said. "Are you a writer?"

"Yes. I suppose I am. As a matter of fact, it's my play they are about to perform here." Tom had picked up the last of the pages, and the man wiped it clean using his sleeve and added it to the pile. "My name is Shakespeare," he said. "Bill Shakespeare. Or Will Shakespeare, if you prefer. Or Bill . . ."

Tom was confused. "Is that with a B or not a B?" he asked.

"B or not a B. B or not a B." Shakespeare's eyes brightened, and he suddenly produced a quill and scribbled something down on one of the pages. "That's rather good," he said. "I might use that."

"What is your play about?" Tom asked, changing the subject. Behind them the second actor had just been dismissed as brutally as the first. A third actor was taking his place.

"Oh. It's about a Roman general called Titus Andronicus," Shakespeare said. "Actually, it's rather violent. But that's what they want. . . ." He pointed at the two men on the stage. "That's Philip Henslowe. He owns the theatre. The other man is Lord Strange . . . and what's really strange is that we work for him at all, because between you and me he's a complete idiot. All he ever wants is clowns and acrobats." He shook his head, then glanced at Tom. "Are you here to audition?" he asked suddenly.

"Yes."

"Oh. I see." Shakespeare grimaced. "I'm sorry to have to say it, but I think they're no longer looking for girls."

"I'm not a girl!" Tom said indignantly.

"No, no, no!" Shakespeare laughed. "That's not

what I meant! Didn't you know? We don't have girls in the theatre. All the girls' parts are played by boys."

This was something that Tom had never known. "Why?" he asked.

"They just are!" Shakespeare searched through the pages. "But as I say, there are only two girls in the play and they are both cast."

"Oh." Tom was downcast. "Isn't there anything else?"

"Nothing that would suit you." Shakespeare sighed. "Why do you want to be an actor anyway?" he asked. "Have you acted before?"

"No."

"But you have been to a play."

"Only once." Suddenly Tom found himself telling Shakespeare about the play he had seen at the Red Lion. As he started to describe the plot, he saw Shakespeare smile and a moment later the playwright laughed and slapped him on the back. "There's no need to tell me about the play," he said. "It was *The Comedy of Errors*. I wrote it."

Tom gasped. "You're a great writer," he said.

"No, no, no!" Shakespeare blushed. "I'm only starting, really. But one day . . . who knows?"

Despite his meeting with Shakespeare, Tom was feeling lost and dejected as he left the theatre. The visit had been a complete failure. There were no parts for him in the play. He had nowhere to go, no money, and no possessions except the clothes he was wearing.

He was so deep in thought that he didn't notice someone slipping out of the theatre behind him. But as he walked down the road, the man hurried after him and finally caught up.

"Excuse me, young sir." The speaker was short and very dark, with narrow, glinting eyes. He was quite bald, apart from two patches of black hair, one above each ear. He also had a mustache, the hairs curling around on each side of his nose. He was dressed exotically in a rich, multicolored tunic with a bright red sash across his chest and a matching red plume in his hat. His trousers were mauve, ballooning out above the knee, where they were tied tightly with two black ribbons. His stockings were also red. His feet, which were extremely small, were encased in brightly polished black shoes. "I noticed you in the theatre just now," the man went on. There was something foreign about him. Although his English was perfect, there was the trace of an accent, distant and unrecognizable to Tom. "You were hoping to perform in a play?"

"Yes." Tom kept on walking.

The man hurried to keep up, almost dancing on his tiny feet. "Then permit me to introduce myself," he said. "My name is Dr. Mobius. You know my name?

No? No matter." He coughed delicately. "The truth is that I myself have a theatrical company."

That stopped Tom in his tracks. The man smiled at him. He was wearing some sort of perfume and smelled of flowers and musk. "We call ourselves The Garden Players." He waved a set of fingers heavy with rings. "We have a play we wish to perform, and I came to the Rose because I am in need of a boy."

"What sort of play is it?" Tom's mind was reeling, and it was the first thing he could think to ask.

Dr. Mobius tweaked his mustache. "It is a comedy," he explained. "A very comical comedy, in my opinion. But then, I wrote it. It is entitled *The Devil and His Boy.* You see? I play the devil. But, due to an unfortunate accident, I find myself lacking a boy."

"And you think . . . ?" Tom tried to make sense of his thoughts. "What makes you think I'd be right for the part?" he asked.

Dr. Mobius simpered. "It is in my skin," he said. "That is, I am a very sensitive person. I can sense talent in a young man like yourself. The way you carry yourself. The way you speak. Of course"—he whipped out a handkerchief and brushed an imaginary tear from his eye—"if you are not interested . . ."

"I am interested!" Tom exclaimed.

"How interesting! Good!" Suddenly he was businesslike. "It will be three weeks' work. We will pay you three shillings in advance and a further three shillings when the job is done. You will live with us, with The Garden Players, and you will receive all food and board." He paused for breath. "What is your name?" he asked.

"Tom. Tom Falconer."

"You are alone in London?"

Tom was about to mention Moll, then thought better of it. She wasn't part of this life. "Yes," he said.

"Then is it agreed?"

Tom hesitated for a moment. Somewhere, deep inside him, Tom knew that there was something wrong, that this was simply too good to be true. After all, the last time he had been offered work, it had nearly cost him both his legs. But at the same time it was a job. A roof over his head. Food. And he would be acting in a play!

"Agreed," he said.

Dr. Mobius stretched out his arm to shake hands, and it was then that it happened. He must have lost a button, because for a moment his sleeve fell away from his arm. Looking down, Tom saw the man's dark skin and there, just above the wrist, a strange mark. It was an eye with a cross in it. And it hadn't been drawn there. It had been burned into his flesh.

The man glanced at Tom, then down to his exposed arm. For a moment his eyes flared and he opened his mouth in what was almost a snarl. But then he forced the smile back onto his face and pulled the sleeve down. "My sleeve," he said. "These London tailors have no idea what they're doing!" He brought his hand back up in front of Tom. "So, Tom Falconer. I am the devil. Are you going to be my boy? If so, let's shake."

Tom reached out.

They shook.

9

The Garden Players

There were eight men in the company known as The Garden Players, but with Tom that figure was brought up to nine.

Tom had followed Dr. Mobius back up the south bank of the river. The sun was still shining brightly, but Tom couldn't help noticing something rather strange. Mobius preferred the shadows. Whenever the street widened out—when they crossed Long Southwark, for example—his beady eyes searched for darkened alleyways and hidden entrances. If he saw people coming toward him, he chose another way. And so they barely saw anyone as they followed the Thames, heading east, past London Bridge and on to Bermondsey.

They finally arrived at the river itself, and Dr. Mobius stopped, blinking in the light. It was snowing now and Tom could see the surface of the Thames beginning to ice over. He wondered how long it would be before he was able to cross it on foot.

"Here we are," Mobius panted, speaking for the first time since they had set off. He waved a hand. "We are here."

"Where . . . ?" Tom began.

The river was lapping at a derelict wooden jetty in front of them. A single ship was moored there, obviously no longer seaworthy. The sails hung in rags from its four masts, and there was a gaping hole in its side where the wood seemed to have moldered away. But there were no buildings close by—no taverns and certainly no theatres.

"The ship, Tom!" Mobius pressed his fingers together. "We hired a ship. To save money, you understand. We live there. We work—the deck is a perfect stage. We are, if you like, a family afloat. Yes, I like that. The family that floats. And now you are part of our family, Tom. A very welcome part. Please! This way. . . ."

Dr. Mobius walked up a half-rotten gangplank, and Tom followed.

"This way!" Mobius pointed at a door and a set of steps leading down inside the ship, and disappeared. Tom stood for a moment, feeling the deck moving underneath his feet. He had never been on a ship before and had no idea how so much wood and rigging could possibly float when even the smallest stone would sink instantly. But this was no time for such questions. Nervous now, he crossed the deck and went through the door.

There were seven men, sitting in chairs or lying in hammocks around a coal brazier. The room was full of smoke both from the fire and from the candles that lit it. Mobius had removed his hat and was helping himself to a glass of sherry from a small wooden cask. "Gentlemen," he said, "our new boy! Yes! His name is Tom. . . ."

The men nodded at Tom, and one or two of them smiled. The first thing that Tom noticed was that like Dr. Mobius, they were all rather dark. The oldest of them must have been about forty, the youngest (playing a woman, as it turned out) only a few years older than Tom himself. They were dressed in leather trousers, thick shirts, and boots. Sitting there, in the cramped and smoky cabin, they looked more like sailors or soldiers than actors.

Mobius introduced them. "This is Ferdinand. Frederick. Philip. Florian. Francis with an i. Frances with an e. And Fynes." Tom promptly forgot each man's name as he was told it and wondered how he would manage when it came to learning his lines. He was beginning to feel more and more uncomfortable. It wasn't that the

men were unfriendly. It was just the way they were looking at him . . . soft and secretive. He had thought actors
would be more cheerful than this.

"We must start work!" Mobius exclaimed. "Ferdinand—a copy for our new friend."

The men swung off their bunks and moved to sit
around a low table in the middle of the cabin. They each
had a great bundle of paper, and one of them produced
a script that he handed to Tom. It was the moment Tom
had been dreading. He turned to Mobius, the blood
rushing to his face. "I can't read," he said.

But to his surprise, Mobius merely laughed. "It does
not matter! We will help you to learn the lines. And when
you have learned the lines, you won't need to read."

The youngest actor—Florian—a boy with long, fair
hair and sad eyes—sat down next to Tom and took his
script. "I will read the lines for you," he said. Like Mobius, he spoke with a slightly foreign accent.

For the next ninety minutes Tom listened as Mobius
and The Garden Players read *The Devil and His Boy*.

The play was, as Mobius had said, a comedy. It was
about a man called Lucio (played by Dr. Mobius), who
had just arrived in the city of Venice and who dressed up
as the devil in order to win a bet. Very quickly, though,
things got out of hand as the people of Venice came to
believe that he was the *real* devil. There was a comical
merchant with a beautiful daughter, Isabella (played by

Florian), a comical priest, and a comical duke. In fact, everyone in the play was meant to be comical in one way or another. The play ended with the duke and two soldiers, all of them armed with muskets, chasing Lucio and his boy off the stage.

The boy, of course, was Tom's part. He played Antonio, Lucio's servant, but as it turned out, this wasn't such a big part after all. Tom appeared in the first three acts and once at the end. His main job was to provide a sort of commentary on the action. "Methinks my master is a scurvy knave"—that sort of thing. But he didn't complain. Listening to the actors reading the play, he still found it hard to believe that he was one of them. It did trouble him a little that the play didn't seem to be very good. And it also occurred to him—although of course he couldn't be sure—that not one of these actors could actually act. They all had that strange, very faint foreign accent. And they seemed to be reading their parts with no interest or enthusiasm whatsoever. But it was a start. The Garden Players today. The Rose Theatre tomorrow. At least, that was what Tom told himself.

They reached the end of the fifth act. Florian turned over the last page. There was a moment's pause, but nobody applauded or said anything to break the silence.

"So are there any questions?" Mobius asked.

Tom waited, but still nobody spoke. There had been a question he had been meaning to ask from the very start, something that had puzzled him. But for the moment it was out of his mind and he asked instead, "When are we going to perform the play?"

"Soon." Mobius sipped his sherry. "I still have a few little arrangements that have to be, you know, arranged."

"It's a lot to learn." This was Florian, who, as Isabella, had one of the largest parts.

"We will work hard." Dr. Mobius set down his glass and stared hard at everyone around the table. "From today, none of us will leave this ship without my permission. We will rehearse on the deck or—if the snow or the rain of this accursed country makes that impossible—down here. Florian! You will teach Tom his lines. Day and night. We must be ready for our grand opening." He turned to Tom. "From now on, Tom, you are mine. You must remember that. Do as you are told. And take care. We would hate anything accidental to happen to you . . . accidentally. You understand?"

Suddenly Tom knew what he had meant to ask before. "The boy who was supposed to play my part . . ." He looked up at Mobius. "What happened to him?"

One of the men shifted uncomfortably on his stool. Next to Tom, Florian cast his eyes down and pretended to study the script. Dr. Mobius sighed and spread his hands, his many rings sparkling in the light of the candles. "Poor Frank," he said. "It is exactly what I mean. Yes. Exactly. You see, he tried to leave the ship one night without asking my permission. Somehow he must have slipped . . . in the dark, maybe." Dr. Mobius laid a hand on Tom's shoulder. He leaned down and gazed straight at him. "He fell into the river and drowned. Make sure the same thing does not happen to you!"

Rehearsals began that afternoon, and for the next three days Tom found himself utterly absorbed in the business of producing a play. Fortunately it had stopped snowing and they were able to rehearse in the morning. The play demanded lots of running around, sometimes with guns, sometimes with devil pitchforks, and Tom wondered how they would ever have managed inside.

Because he relied on Florian to read his lines, he found himself closer to the other boy than to anyone else. The rest of the company were as reserved as they had been when he first met them. They rarely spoke to him. But nor did they often speak to each other. They seemed nervous. He wondered if any of them had ever acted before.

It wasn't easy getting Florian to talk either. As the days passed, he learned that the boy was sixteen years old and that Dr. Mobius was his uncle.

"When did you start acting?" Tom asked.

"This is my first play."

"Is it something you always wanted to do?"

"No!" Florian fell silent, his sad eyes turning away.

"I just do what my uncle tells me to," he said. "Now stop asking questions and we will read through your lines."

Tom was perplexed. But it was only on his third night on the boat that he saw something that actually disturbed him.

All the actors slept in one room—the same room where they had read the play. This was the only room on the ship that was remotely dry or warm enough, except for Dr. Mobius's private cabin on the other side of the deck. Tom had a hammock next to Florian, with the actor called Ferdinand (who played the merchant) on the other side. However, that night Tom couldn't sleep. The weather was colder than ever, the river a solid sheet of ice now. He could feel the chill in the moonlight that was seeping through the cracks in the woodwork, creeping into his bones.

Next to him Ferdinand groaned and turned over. As he did so, his shirt sleeve got caught and pulled back, and it was then that Tom saw it. An eye with a cross. Burned into the man's flesh between his wrist and his elbow. He had seen exactly the same thing on the arm of Dr. Mobius.

Tom straightened up. What did it mean? Were *all* the actors carrying the same mark? And if so, why? Why should they have consented to allow themselves to be branded like animals?

Tom lay back down in his hammock and closed his eyes. But that night he didn't sleep a wink.

Another day came and went. Tom had learned all of acts 1 and 2, and most of act 3. That only left a short scene in act 5 and he would be ready. But ready for what? Dr. Mobius still hadn't said where or when *The Devil and His Boy* was going to be performed. And Tom still hadn't been paid. He had tried asking Florian, but of course without success, and was just summoning up the courage to tackle Dr. Mobius himself when the visitor arrived.

It was about four o'clock in the afternoon and already dark, a few flurries of snow gusting against the rotting boat. Tom was watching a scene from act 4 being rehearsed when the man approached the ship. He was wearing a long brown robe that reached all the way to his feet, with a hood drawn over his head. A monk or a friar. The man glanced over his shoulder, then hurried up the gangplank. At that moment Dr. Mobius saw him. "That is, I think, sufficient for today," he called out, stopping the rehearsal in midsentence. "Please return to your cabin. Yes, I think, to the cabin. While I attend to some . . . business."

The monk had stood waiting while Mobius spoke. Then Mobius bowed and gestured toward his private quarters on the other side of the deck. Still keeping his face hidden underneath the hood, the monk scuttled across the deck and disappeared through the door. Dr. Mobius followed him. The door slammed shut behind them.

The other actors were only too pleased to be released from their work in the cold evening air and crowded around the door in their haste to get back to the fire. Florian went with them, and suddenly Tom, who had been sitting on the deck above, found himself alone and momentarily forgotten.

His first instinct was to follow the others down. It was extremely cold, and the last one in would always find himself farthest from the fire. But at the same time he was curious. Why should a monk have suddenly chosen to visit a company of actors, and why should Dr. Mobius be so eager to see him? He had to know. And perhaps there was a way he could find out.

There was a rope lying on the deck. In fact, there were ropes all over the ship, but this was the only one that hadn't been gnawed at either by time or by rats. Tom snatched it up and tied it around one of the masts, lowering the other end into the river. Then, taking hold of the rope, he lifted himself over the railing that ran the full length of the deck and began to lower himself down the side.

Dr. Mobius's cabin was directly below him and a little to one side. Hanging in space with his arms outstretched, his feet up against the side of the ship, and his head hanging back, Tom was able to maneuver himself until he could look through the window into the cabin. He was about three yards below the deck and three yards above the frozen water of the Thames. If he let go of the rope, he knew that he would fall right through the ice. It still wasn't strong enough to support his weight. But it might be strong enough to trap him underneath the surface. Tom imagined himself in the chill black water. He thought about the boy whose place he had taken. Would he have frozen before he drowned? Which would have killed him first?

Clinging on even tighter now, Tom looked into the cabin. The first thing he saw was that the monk wasn't a monk at all. He had taken off his robe, and underneath he was dressed like a gentleman, with a white collar, a black velvet cape, black stockings, and black boots. The man had a beard and a mustache, both turning gray. His eyes were narrow and slightly too small for his head. His nose, long and hooked, was slightly too big for it. There was a thin, tapering scar on the side of his cheek shaped like the letter J. From where Tom was hanging, he could also see a table, a chair, candles, and a bed against the wall. But Dr. Mobius himself was just out of sight.

". . . the gold? I haven't come all the way across London to leave without it."

It was the "monk" talking. With a thrill of excitement, Tom realized that he could hear every word the two men were saying. The cabin window might have had glass once, but it had been broken or had rotted away long ago. Tom eased himself closer, gently shifting his weight on his feet. He had to be careful. Move too quickly and he might find himself accidentally knocking on their wall.

"Of course I have the gold," Mobius replied. A cloth bag appeared, thrown down on the table. It landed with a heavy clink. "But what I want to know, what you must tell me is"—his hand fell on the bag before the other man could take it—"do you have what *I* want?"

"It's not easy, damn you," the man muttered. "I'm doing my best. I'm sticking my neck out for you. Literally! I could lose my head for this!"

"But you're not doing it for me," Mobius purred. He lifted the bag again. "You are doing it for this. You are going to be very, very wealthy."

"If anyone finds out, I'm going to be very, very dead."

"They won't."

The man in black stood up and walked over to the window. Outside, Tom twisted away, afraid he was going to be discovered. For a nightmare moment he lost his footing and hung upside down, his neck twisted and a sky of black ice filling his vision. But the man had turned around. Tom managed to loop the rope over his foot. He was still upside down. But he was safe.

"What about this new boy?" the man asked. "Who is he?"

"He's nobody. Nothing. A creature I picked out of the gutter." Mobius purred quietly, and Tom could imagine him stroking his curling mustache.

"He suspects nothing?"

"Of course not. He'll play his part and then we'll be rid of him. But we were speaking of you, Sir Richard. When will I have a result?"

"Tomorrow. Maybe the day after. They're meeting soon. . . ."

"You can take half the gold now. Half later. And don't disappoint me, Sir Richard." There was a brief pause and Dr. Mobius moved closer. Tom could just make out the side of his face and part of his body. One eye gleamed in the candlelight. "I have far-reaching friends. You may hide from me, but not from them."

Tom sensed that the interview was coming to an end and quickly pulled himself back up the side of the boat. He thought of the rope stretching out across the deck. He couldn't risk Dr. Mobius or the man he had called Sir Richard finding it.

There was nobody in sight on the deck. Tom climbed over the railing and untied the rope. He was just straightening up when a hand fell on his shoulder. Tom froze, then turned softly.

Florian was standing over him. For a moment neither

of them spoke. Tom wondered if the other boy was going to raise the alarm. He must have seen what Tom had been doing. He must know what Tom had overheard.

But then Florian began to speak, the words tumbling out as a whisper on a frosting cloud of breath. Tom couldn't understand what he was saying. The words made no sense. He shook his head, tried to interrupt, but Florian wouldn't stop. At last he seemed to realize what he was doing. He paused and grabbed hold of Tom's arms.

"Tom," he said, "I like you. But you have to go. Don't you see? You're in terrible danger. You must get off this ship. Leave London. Go as far away as you can."

A door banged open. Mobius was showing the "monk" back to the shore. Florian turned and fled the other way. Tom stepped into the shadows, his mind whirling.

He had barely understood a word of what Florian had said. And it wasn't just because Tom had been taken by surprise or because all the blood had rushed to his head when he was upside down. No. Florian had spoken to him for a minute, maybe for longer. But whatever language he had been speaking, it certainly wasn't English.

10

Thin Ice

There were no rehearsals on Christmas Day. Tom asked if he could leave the ship and was pleasantly surprised when Dr. Mobius said yes. In fact, Mobius seemed quite keen for him to take a day's holiday.

Tom was glad to get back on dry land. He walked for twenty minutes—it was easy to find his way. All he had to do was follow the river back down to London Bridge. Soon he was recognizing familiar landmarks. And it was just before midday when he found himself in front of the shoe shop over which Moll Cutpurse lived.

He was about to call up to her when Moll came out. She stopped and stared at him, and although she did her best to hide it, Tom knew that she was pleased to see him.

"You've come back!" She scowled.

"You did say I could look in on Christmas Day," Tom replied.

Moll softened. "Oh, yes. Happy Christmas." She ran her eye over him. "Well, you haven't been starving, I can see that," she said. "So can I take it you're an actor now?"

"Yes. I'm in a play!"

"Tried on the dress yet?" She smiled. "You'll look nice with your lips painted. In fact, you'll probably make a much better girl than me." Somewhere in the distance a church clock chimed the hour. It was eleven o'clock. "I was just on my way to a Christmas feast," Moll continued. "You're not invited, but as they're all thieves and vagabonds, I don't suppose they'll complain."

It was one of the strangest invitations Tom had ever received, although of course it was also the only invitation he'd ever received. Christmas in Framlingham had only ever meant extra work. "Thank you," he said.

Moll headed back through Southwark and past the great bull-baiting ring at Bankside. The other side of the river was heavily built up, but on this side the buildings suddenly stopped, giving way first to gardens and then to open fields. The snow had fallen thicker here. To the south everything was white, with only a few cows standing out against the landscape. Ahead of them a single inn stood at the edge of a clump of trees. Moll went up to the door and knocked. The door opened a crack and a pair of dark eyes gazed suspiciously out.

"Moll!" a voice exclaimed.

The door opened fully, and Moll and Tom went in.

It was a small inn, but it was packed with about twenty or thirty people sitting at a long table and chattering among themselves. As soon as they saw Moll and Tom, they bustled about making a space at the table so that the two new arrivals could sit down.

"Let me introduce you," Moll said to Tom. "That's Black Bob." She pointed at a man who was actually rather pale. "He's a highwayman. And so is One-Eyed Jack. . . ." She pointed to a second man. "Snatcher Sam and Old Shagbag, there at the end of the table. Dick the Dealer there is a cardsharp." She nodded at a man with a little pointy mustache and the man waved back, suddenly producing a pack of cards out of nowhere in his empty hand. "Over there are the Bird Brothers."

"London's finest burglars," the brothers—two plump men in identical green doublets—chorused in unison.

And then Tom remembered what Moll had said. "They're all thieves and vagabonds. . . ." She had been telling the truth. *Everyone* at the inn was crooked in one way or another. There were more pickpockets, several confidence tricksters, a passport forger, two horse thieves, two hookers, two curbers, and two divers. Tom wasn't sure what all these actually did, but they certainly looked very villainous, with squinting eyes and wide, toothless smiles. It felt a bit strange to be the only person in the room who hadn't committed some sort of crime, but then the food arrived and he soon found himself joining in the party with all his doubts forgotten.

It was a wonderful Christmas meal. There was a peacock pie, a goose, and a pair of ducks. A whole boar's head arrived, chewing on an apple and even managing to look fairly cheerful, considering it was being served up on a wooden plate. When that was all gone, there was a pudding—a model of the Tower of London made entirely out of marzipan—that was carried into the room to cheers and applause. Finally, there were hot chestnuts and more mulled ale, and then someone brought out a fiddle and everyone began to sing, although, unfortunately, not the same song.

Nobody had minded Tom being there, and during the meal the cardsharp had shown him how to strip out an ace, and one of the confidence tricksters had tried to sell him London Bridge. But he had spent most of the time telling Moll about The Garden Players. He also told her about some of the mysteries of the past few days—the man with the scar who had come to the boat, Florian's warning, and the strange marks on the arms of Dr. Mobius and the actor called Ferdinand. Moll had made no comment about any of this, but her eyes narrowed, and as the meal went on, she became quiet and thoughtful.

Outside, the sun was beginning to set, and Tom realized it was time to go. He got up and slipped out the door. Moll came with him, and the two of them stood for a minute in the dying light.

"Thank you, Moll," Tom said. He suddenly felt guilty. "I have no money," he added. "How can I pay for my food?"

"I'll pay for you," Moll said. "You can pay me back when you're a famous actor."

They shook hands. Tom was about to leave, but Moll stopped him. "The Garden Players . . ." she said suddenly.

"What about them?"

"Nothing about them sounds quite right. A comedy that isn't funny. Dr. Mobius. The way they employed you without even hearing you read." She scowled. "When that boy, Florian, spoke to you, you said he was talking in a foreign language. Do you know what language it was?"

Tom shook his head. "Not English. . . ."

"Could it have been French? Or Dutch?"

"I don't know, Moll."

"No. You wouldn't." Moll sighed. Inside the tavern there was a peal of laughter and clapping from the rest of the assembly. "I must go in," Moll said. "But remember, Tom, if you find yourself in trouble, you only have to ask for me by name. Ask anyone—a beggar, a street-boy, a porter, a water-carrier. Just tell them to fetch Moll Cutpurse. They'll know where to find me."

"I'm not in trouble . . ." Tom began.

"Not yet. But you might be." Moll shook her head, then turned around and went back into the inn.

Tom walked away. "I'm not in trouble," he had said. But he hadn't even taken ten paces and he was.

Someone stepped out from behind a tree. The blade of a knife flashed in what was left of the fading sunlight. A hand reached out and grabbed him roughly by the shirt, twisting him around.

"Good afternoon, Tom-Tom," Gamaliel Ratsey said in a soft, singsong voice. "I thought I might find you here."

"Ratsey!"

"My dear fellow! I am so glad to see you." Ratsey touched the point of the knife against Tom's neck. "Happy Christmas, by the way."

"How did you find me?"

"Oh, I heard that you and Moll—what's her name?— Cut-throat had teamed up, so I've been keeping an eye on her. She led me here." He shivered. "Jolly cold, Tom-Tom. Deadly cold, you might say."

"What do you want with me?"

"I would have thought it was obvious. The truth is, you rather let us down, running off like that. The Slopes were very disappointed."

"I will not go back to Framlingham!"

Ratsey smiled and waved the point of his dagger in a

circle around Tom's head. "You're not going anywhere," he said.

"You're going to kill me!"

"It does rather look as if I'm going to have to," Ratsey agreed. "It saddens me, Tom. But you know too much about me."

"I won't tell on you, Ratsey," Tom pleaded. "I have a new life now, in London. I'm an actor. You can forget about me." He took a step back, trying to buy time, desperately searching for the right words. He had always been afraid of Ratsey and knew him for the killer that he was. But he wondered if there wasn't some way he could appeal to him. Surely there had to be some good in the man? "You can't just kill me in cold blood," he went on. "You're not like that. . . ."

"But I am." Ratsey sighed and for a moment he looked genuinely sad.

"No! You were a soldier. Captain Ratsey! You told me so yourself. You fought for the queen!"

"And what did the queen ever do for me?" His eyes blazed. "Oh, yes, I was once like you, Tom-Tom. A nice boy. A good boy. Fighting for the queen to save the country. But when the fighting was over and the battle was won, what happened? They gave me nothing! No pension. No reward. I was abandoned, left to starve, all on my own. . . ."

"You had parents. . . ."

"I had run away from home. They no longer wanted to know me. There was no one to look after poor old Ratsey, so I had to learn to look after myself. And that is what I am doing now, Tom-Tom. I like you. Yes, I do. But, you see, you know too much. And maybe one day you'll whisper a few words . . . just by accident. Maybe in your sleep! I can't let that happen. I can't take the risk."

It was no good. Tom glanced left and right. They were standing in an open field, underneath a tree. Thick snow lay all around them and in the branches above. There was nobody in sight. Ratsey had led him away from the inn and Tom knew that even if he did call for help, he would be dead long before anyone arrived. Suddenly he felt very cold. Despite his new boots, the snow was reaching up to his ankles, penetrating into his bones. The wind blew and a trickle of snow fell out of the tree and onto his neck.

The snow . . .

"So let's get this finished with," Ratsey said. "I'm sorry, Tom. I hope you understand—it's nothing personal."

"Wait a minute, Ratsey!" Tom brought his hands together as if to plead for mercy. He was hoping he *had* learned something about acting in the last few days. "You can't kill me. I'm only a child!"

"It's never stopped me before. . . ."

"But I'm unarmed. . . ." Now Tom turned his palms upward. "Look! I have no weapon." Slowly Tom raised his arms.

"Most of the people I kill have no weapons," Ratsey said reasonably. "It makes it a lot easier." His fingers tightened on the knife. "Now stop all this nonsense, Tom-Tom. The time has come!"

Tom's hands were now over his head. There was a branch directly above him. His hands closed over it and with all his strength he pulled down.

A great clump of snow fell out of the tree, both onto Tom and onto Ratsey in front of him. Tom had been ready for it. Ratsey hadn't. Ratsey cursed, momentarily blinded. At the same moment Tom turned and ran.

He was only seconds ahead of Ratsey. The highwayman had recovered fast and, scooping the snow out of his eyes, had launched himself after Tom. It was a strange, soundless pursuit. They were running almost in slow motion as their feet came down in the thick snow, and even the sound of Tom's rasping breath was smothered by the frozen air.

Tom had no idea where he was going, but realized—when it was too late—that he had managed to curve away from the inn where he might have found help. As he stumbled through the snow, almost slipping, scrabbling forward, he caught sight of a group of people weaving slowly down a lane. Should he make for them? No. It

was hopeless. They were probably half-drunk, and before
he could even begin to explain what was happening, Ratsey would have cut his throat.

"Tom . . . !"

He must have slowed down. Ratsey had almost
caught up with him. The knife flashed through the air,
and Tom cried out as the very tip of it caught him on the
shoulders, slicing through his shirt and drawing a line
across his skin. The pain and the shock of it propelled
him forward. Ratsey stumbled and almost lost his balance. Tom surged ahead.

He reached a row of houses, found an alleyway, and
ran through it. But it was then that he made his fatal mistake. Even as he ran forward he looked back. His legs
had carried him the next ten yards before he knew what
he had done, and by the time he saw where he was, it was
too late.

He was near Bankside. Without realizing it, he had
entered a long wooden jetty stretching out into the
river Thames. Unfortunately the jetty only continued
for another twenty yards and stopped. It was a passage
to nowhere, and before Tom could double back and regain dry land, Ratsey had reached the other end, block-
ing it.

The man and the boy stopped and stood there, gazing at each other. Ratsey was breathing heavily. His dark
hair had flopped across his face, and he threw his head

back to clear it. His eyes, when they were revealed, were alight with pleasure.

"You move fast, Tom-Tom," he panted.

"Leave me alone, Ratsey." Tom took two paces back. Two paces closer to the end of the jetty and the river Thames.

Ratsey lifted the knife and took another step forward. The jetty creaked underneath him.

"Tom, Tom, the piper's son"—Ratsey had begun to sing—"cannot hide and he cannot run."

Tom had reached the end of the jetty. A wooden ladder led down to the Thames, but there were no boats. Ratsey was getting closer. And then, in an instant, Tom knew what he had to do. Without taking his eyes off Ratsey, he grabbed hold of the ladder and lowered himself down. . . .

Not into water. Onto ice.

Ratsey stared for a moment, then darted forward. But he was already too late. Tom had backed away, wobbling uncertainly, but still standing upright on the ice.

"Come back!" Ratsey squealed. His eyes flared, and slipping the knife between his teeth, he turned and launched himself down the ladder. But his feet had barely touched the ice when there was a sudden crack, and with a shuddering scream he disappeared into a gaping hole that had suddenly appeared beneath him. If he hadn't been holding on to the ladder he would have been sucked into the black, freezing water. As it was, he barely had the strength to pull himself out, and by the time he was back on top of the jetty, his teeth were rattling with cold.

"T-T-T-Tom!" he tried to call out. Tom was standing only a few yards away, but now they could have been a world apart. "C-c-come back!" Ratsey grabbed hold of himself as if trying to squeeze out the icy water. He no longer had the knife. He must have dropped it when he plunged into the river. "The ice! It won't hold your weight!"

"No thanks!" Tom slid backward, not daring to lift his feet off the ice. He could feel it straining under his weight. Nobody else had tried to cross the Thames yet. It had been cold, but not cold enough. The ice was thin. In places it was almost transparent, with the water oozing blackly through. But Tom was certain about one thing. He would sooner disappear through the ice and drown than go back to the jetty and face Ratsey again.

He kept walking. He didn't need to look back at Ratsey to know he wasn't being followed. He was a boy, small and underweight, and the ice was only just supporting him. Ratsey, as he had already proved, had no chance. Tom took another three paces, then cried out as the ice gave away beneath him. One of his feet shot through into the water, which closed around his ankle, instantly sucking out any feeling at all. Tom twisted sideways. Fortunately the ice was stronger here. With his foot dripping, he fought for balance and found it. For a moment he stood in the middle of the river, wondering which way to go, wondering if he could even find the courage to move.

Hunching his shoulders against the wind, which was whipping up the river from Westminster, Tom continued across. It was much colder than he had thought. Out in the open, with nothing to protect him, his whole body was quickly growing numb. It was also much farther than he would have liked. After ten minutes on the ice he wasn't even halfway to the other side. A fist of loose snow punched into his face, forcing him to close his eyes. When he looked back, he could no longer see Ratsey. The highwayman must have given him up for lost.

He pressed on. The ice groaned and creaked, but gradually the buildings on the other side of the river loomed ahead of him, almost invisible in the darkness. Another wooden jetty twisted out, water lapping at its legs. He took another step. The ice cracked. He yelled out and toppled forward, his arms flying out. Somehow his hands caught hold of wood. One leg disappeared into the water, soaking and freezing him all the way up to the thigh. But then he was out, pulling himself up onto the jetty. Behind him, shards of ice closed over the hole he had just made. More snow fell.

But he'd made it. He was safe.

◆ ◆ ◆

It was nighttime before he got back to the ship where The Garden Players were housed. It had taken him two hours to get there, partly because he was cold and exhausted, partly because he had been afraid of bumping into Ratsey. Although it was Christmas, the night watchmen were still out. He glimpsed one of them crossing a bridge with a lantern held up in front of him, and he heard the familiar cry:

> *Eight o'clock, look well to your locks,*
> *Your fire and your light. God give you good night.*

The night still held one final surprise.

Tom had just gotten back to Bermondsey and was approaching the boat when he saw a man leaving, coming down the gangplank. The man came close to him, and although he didn't see Tom, Tom recognized him by the monk's hood and robe he was wearing. It was the man with the scar, the one that Dr. Mobius had called Sir Richard. The man hurried off into the night. Tom waited until he had gone, then walked over to the gangplank and went up onto the boat.

He had hoped to make it to the cabin without being seen, but he had barely moved before a door opened and Dr. Mobius appeared, climbing up from below.

"Tom?" Dr. Mobius had a glass of wine in one hand,

a pipe in the other. His cabin was lit by the soft yellow glow of a candle. He stepped out onto the deck.

"I have some good tidings!" Dr. Mobius stretched out a hand, his rings glinting in the candlelight. He laid it gently on Tom's head, stroking his hair. "We are to perform *The Devil and His Boy* in three days' time."

"That's wonderful," Tom said.

"It is better than you think, my dear friend. We have been greatly honored. Yes, indeed, it is an honor. The performance is to take place in the palace of White-hall."

"A palace?" Tom's mind was beginning to spin—but there was more to come.

"Yes, Tom." His lips curled in a slow smile and something brighter than candlelight gleamed in his eyes. "In Whitehall Palace. And we'll be performing in front of the queen."

11

First Night Nerves

The next three days were a whirlwind of activity. There were still lines to be learned, movements to be discussed, fights to be choreographed, and costumes to be sewn. And then there were the props and scenery. Like most plays, *The Devil and His Boy* didn't need much scenery—the audience was expected to imagine it—but there were a lot of props, and it was one of these that led to a strange and unpleasant incident.

The prop was a pitchfork.

Tom was rehearsing on the deck in the cold morning sunlight. The entire cast was there, some of them acting, the rest sewing or painting. Florian, he noticed, was looking very downcast. In fact, the older boy had barely spoken a word to him since the night of the warning. However, he noticed Florian glance upward sharply as Dr. Mobius appeared from his cabin, carrying the two pitchforks.

"This is for you, Tom," Dr. Mobius said. "When you disguise yourself as a devil, this is what you must carry. Please handle it with great care."

The pitchfork was about two yards long, and taking it, Tom was surprised by its weight. Examining it, he soon realized why it was so heavy. The actual prongs themselves were only wood, but the length of the pitch-fork was a hollow metal tube—if it hadn't been for the prongs, glued to the top, Tom would have been able to look right through it. There was one other slightly strange thing. At the end of the tube, on the inside, some sort of line had been cut. Tom ran his thumb over it, feeling the sharp metal edge pressing into his flesh. Obviously the metal tube had been used for something before it had been turned into a fork. But why hadn't Dr. Mobius used a broom handle or even a roll of paper? It would have been lighter and easier to handle.

It was while they were running around the deck that Tom dropped his pitchfork. The wooden forks snapped off and the metal tube began to roll along the deck.

Everyone froze. The tube was heading toward the very edge of the ship. There were no railings there. There was nothing between the tube and the river. And then Florian reacted. Acting as if his life depended on it, he dived forward, throwing himself full-length onto the deck. His outstretched hand caught the tube inches away from the edge. He stood up, holding it.

Dr. Mobius had watched all this with wide eyes. Tom could see the relief in his eyes as Florian lifted the tube, but in seconds relief had been replaced with fury. His whole face seemed to change. His skin grew darker, the veins standing out on his bald head. His mouth drew back in a snarl and the next thing Tom knew his hand had lashed out, crashing into the side of Tom's face and throwing him sprawling onto the deck. With his head spinning he tried to stand up, but Dr. Mobius was already there, looming over him.

"You idiot!" Dr. Mobius shouted. "You fool! I told you to be careful and you almost lost it!"

"It's only a tube of metal!" Tom protested.

"What?" Dr. Mobius drew back his foot and Tom was sure he was going to kick him where he lay. But then Florian sprang forward.

"It was an accident," he said. "You don't have to hurt him!"

Dr. Mobius stared at his nephew with murder in his eyes. For his part, Florian held his ground, the rod still in his hand. Slowly Dr. Mobius recovered. He looked down. Tom was still on his knees. There was a trickle of blood coming from the side of his mouth. Dr. Mobius drew a hand over his eyes as if trying to wipe away the memory of what had just occurred.

"You must forgive me," he said. "That was . . . unforgivable of me." He whipped out his handkerchief and offered it to Tom. Tom didn't take it. "You see," he went on, "to play in front of the queen is a considerable honor. And of course . . . I am nervous. We are all nervous. And this"—he gestured at the metal tube, then at Tom—"it was first night nerves. I apologize to you. It will not happen again." He took the metal rod from Florian and stepped back. "We shall all take a rest," he exclaimed to the watching actors. "We will start again after the midday meal."

The actors dispersed. Tom looked for Florian, but the other boy had already turned away and gone downstairs. Suddenly resolved, Tom got up and followed him.

He found Florian in the costumes room, already at work on the dress that he himself would wear. Tom paused in the doorway. He caught sight of himself in a piece of broken mirror leaning against the wall. There was still a little blood beside his mouth and he wiped it away with his sleeve.

"Thank you," he said.

"That's all right." Florian didn't look up from his work.

"Florian"—Tom moved farther into the room—"the other night . . . last week. You told me I should leave the ship. You said that I was in danger. What did you mean?"

The other boy turned his head away. The dress he was working on was bunched up in his hands. Tom could almost feel him struggling with himself. But then another of the actors appeared at the door and looked in. "Lunch is ready," he said, and went on his way.

Maybe Florian had been about to tell Tom something, but the moment had been interrupted and now the spell was broken. "I didn't mean anything," he said. "I shouldn't have said it. Forget it."

He got up and, brushing past Tom, quickly left the room.

The opening performance of the first night drew closer and closer. They ran through the play once, then again, this time with costumes as well as props. Florian had been transformed into a girl with a flowing dress, makeup, and a wig. Watching him, Tom remembered his meeting with Will Shakespeare and wondered if he could have acted as a girl at the Rose. In his heart he knew he could. He also knew—although it made him sad—that he would much rather be acting in Shakespeare's new play than in *The Devil and His Boy*.

The last morning came and went. Everyone knew their lines. The musicians knew their tunes. They performed the play one last time, and this time Dr. Mobius loaded the muskets so as he and Tom were chased off the stage (this was the last scene of the play) there were loud explosions and puffs of smoke behind them.

Dr. Mobius was pleased with the effect. "It will give Her Majesty much pleasure. The explosions and the alarms." He rolled his mustache between two fingers. "Everyone enjoys that in a play. The last act has to be the best!"

That afternoon they left the ship. A horse and cart had arrived and all the props, costumes, stage furniture, and scripts were carried across in trunks and loaded up in the back. Tom was already feeling dry-mouthed, and wondered what he would be like when they arrived at Whitehall Palace.

When everything had been loaded, he and Florian climbed into the back. There was room for the two boys and for Dr. Mobius at the front of the cart—but everyone else would have to walk. They stood waiting in the cold for a few minutes. Dr. Mobius was the last to leave the ship. He looked briefly in the back of the cart.

"Are you ready?" he asked.

"Yes, Dr. Mobius."

"Then onward . . . to glory!"

Dr. Mobius climbed into the front of the cart, and a moment later they felt a jolt as the cart moved off. Tom glanced back. And it was then that he saw something moving on the deck. It was smoke. It was coming up from below, creeping over the deck and curling around the masts. At first he thought he must be mistaken, but then a tongue of flame shot out, licked at part of the old rigging, and suddenly the whole ship was ablaze.

Tom cried out, but Florian leaned over and stopped him. "It's all right, Tom," he said. "We are finished here. We will not be returning."

The cart rumbled on. The entire ship was ablaze, huge flames reaching up to the very top of the masts. As damp as the ship was, the fire seemed to fall on it like a hungry animal, tearing into it, consuming it utterly. The wood cracked and splintered. One of the masts shivered and fell. The flames leapt up. The ice on the river, glowing red now, began to move, pulling away from the doomed vessel. Slowly the old ship folded in on itself.

And then the cart turned a corner and Tom saw no more.

Whitehall Palace was quite unlike anything Tom had dreamed of. He had imagined a single building, but as the cart passed the great monument at Charing Cross and trundled underneath the arches of the Holbein Gate, he realized that it was an entire town in its own right. There were soaring chapels and tall, solid towers. Elegant stables and neat, compact houses. The whole complex was set in gardens and orchards spread out on the northern bank of the Thames. Tom found it hard to believe that only a few days before he had been close by, fighting for his life on the fragile ice.

They were stopped by a soldier dressed in a red and black tunic with a sword at his waist and an odd weapon—part spear and part axe—on his shoulder. Sitting at the front of the cart, Dr. Mobius produced a letter and handed it to him, and the soldier directed them to a large building that was being guarded by two more similarly dressed men. The cart rolled across the last few yards and Tom got out. The two men seemed to take no notice of him. Passing between them, Tom went in and found himself in the Banqueting Hall, where the play was to be performed.

It was a huge space, at least a hundred yards long, held up by slim wooden pillars garlanded with dried flowers and fruit. The walls seemed to be solid stone, but looking more closely Tom was thrilled to realize that the whole building was a trick. The walls were actually made of canvas. What he was standing in was nothing more than a gigantic tent. But what a tent! The ceiling had been painted as if it were the sky—at one end there were silver stars and a moon, at the other a golden sun, shooting out its beams. At least three hundred glass lamps hung inside, and wreaths of holly and ivy hung everywhere.

A stage had been constructed at one end of the Banqueting Hall. It stood against a screen, behind which the actors could hide when they needed to change or were waiting to come on. There were a number of chairs at the other end, one of them larger than the rest and richly padded with velvet and cushions. Tom didn't need to ask who would be sitting here.

Dr. Mobius had already started carrying in the costumes and props. Tom wondered if he ought to help, but before he could move, there was the sound of stamping feet and a dozen soldiers suddenly marched in, forming a line on either side of the entrance. There was a brief pause and then three more men came in, these wearing brilliantly colored slashed doublets and caps, tight stockings, and highly polished shoes.

Dr. Mobius stopped what he was doing and bowed low. The actors did the same. Tom hesitated for a moment, then remembered himself and bowed as well. The man standing in the middle—he also had some sort of chain of office around his neck and carried a white staff—gestured at Dr. Mobius, who straightened up.

"My name is Edmund Tilney," he said. "I am master in the office of the revels. You are . . ." He creased his brow and glanced at the younger man on his left.

"The Garden Players," the younger man said.

"Quite. And the name of the play you are to perform?"

"The Devil and His Boy," Dr. Mobius told him.

"Oh, yes." The master of the revels frowned. "Not

an entirely suitable title, I feel," he snapped. "But Sir Richard says he found it most enjoyable."

At the mention of Sir Richard, Tom glanced up. He had barely noticed the third man when he came in, but now he saw that it was indeed the same Sir Richard who had come—twice—to the boat. There were the narrow eyes and slightly hooked nose. And there—impossible to miss—was the scar shaped like a J, cut on the side of his cheek.

But even as he stood there uncomfortably with his back bent down and his neck craning up, Tom's mind began to race. As far as he knew *The Devil and His Boy* had never been performed before. Certainly all the actors had had to learn it from scratch. So how could Sir Richard claim to have seen it?

And why had Sir Richard come to the boat, not only at night but in disguise? He remembered seeing Dr. Mobius give him a bag full of coins. What had the money been for?

And, most strange of all, why were Dr. Mobius and Sir Richard pretending they didn't know each other? It wasn't just that they hadn't greeted each other. They weren't even looking each other in the eye.

What exactly was going on?

"Very well," Tilney was saying. "The play will begin at eight o'clock, after Her Majesty has finished supper. There are certain rules that you would be wise to obey."

He cast his eyes over the entire company. "None of you are to look at Her Majesty. If she enjoys the play, she may come and speak to you afterward. If she doesn't, I can assure you that she's the *last* person you would wish to meet. Do not stare at her. Do not attempt to speak to her. You may find it easier just to imagine she is not here."

He paused for breath. From the way he spoke, Tom imagined that he had done this many times before.

"Now, we have to consider the content of this play. I understand it is a comedy. I hope it has jokes."

"The very finest, my lord," Dr. Mobius said, bowing again.

"Good. Her Majesty enjoys a laugh. If you do not hear her laughing, I suggest you finish it as quickly as you can. Leave out acts three and four if you have to." He turned to Sir Richard. "There is nothing vulgar in it, is there?" he asked.

"No, my lord," Sir Richard replied.

"Nothing offensive, sacrilegious, unpatriotic, or treasonable? I have to remind you that the bishop of Winchester is in tonight, and you know how touchy he can be. The devil in this play—we're not talking about Satan, I hope?"

"It is not the real devil, my lord," Dr. Mobius said.

"Good. Good. Good. Now, let me see." He gestured at Sir Richard. "Sir Richard here is the clerk comptroller. If all goes well, he will pay you ten pounds once the play is done. If Her Majesty walks out halfway, it will be five pounds. Is that understood?"

Everyone who had stopped bowing bowed again.

"Now, there's one last item," Tilney said. "Sir Richard informs me that you fire muskets in the last act."

"They are fake muskets," Dr. Mobius exclaimed. "I can assure my lord that Her Majesty will be entertained and not alarmed. . . ."

"Yes! Yes! Yes!" Tilney interrupted. "All your props and luggage will be searched by the Gentlemen Pensioners before she arrives." He gestured at the men in red. "They will search every one of you too. But I think I had better examine these muskets of yours myself."

Dr. Mobius nodded and two of the actors carried forward the trunk that contained the two muskets. They opened it and handed the weapons to Tilney, who glanced at them briefly. "As you will see, my lord," Mobius explained, "the barrels of the guns are fashioned from wood. They are also solid. No ball could pass through them. The only part of the weapon that is authentic is the firing mechanism. We require this to make the . . . small explosions, which, I can assure, my lord, will add a delightful frisson to Her Majesty's evening."

Tilney nodded and set the weapons down. "Very good." He nodded at the Gentlemen Pensioners. "Make sure they are all thoroughly searched."

It took over an hour to search everyone and everything. The Gentlemen Pensioners were the queen's personal bodyguards and it was their job to ensure that nothing remotely dangerous came anywhere near her. Even a small knife that Mobius used to sharpen his quill was removed. The muskets were examined again and set down on a table along with the pitchforks, the devil horns, and all the other bits and pieces from the play. Only when they were completely satisfied did the Gentlemen Pensioners leave, and even then two of them remained behind to guard the door and make sure that nobody else tried to enter.

For the next three hours Tom helped get the stage ready, constructing the scenery, setting out the furniture, and ensuring that everything was in its right place. All the props and costumes had to be carried behind the screen and arranged out-of-sight. The instruments had to be tuned. And finally there were hurried consultations, with the actors whispering their lines to one another, making sure there was nothing they had forgotten. During all this, Tom noticed, Florian didn't say a word. Once Tom tried to speak to him, but the other boy hurriedly broke away as if he were afraid of catching—or giving Tom—the plague.

At last everything was ready. Someone had brought the players some bread, some cold meat, and wine, but everyone was too nervous to eat. Dr. Mobius, however, poured himself a cup of wine and held it up in a toast.

"Today," he said, "is the day that we make history." All the actors were gathered around listening. They seemed to share the same strange gleam in their eyes. Only Florian looked sick and kept his head down. "The twenty-eighth of December, 1593. It is a day that no one in England will forget. It is a day that will belong to the Garduna." He blinked and then turned to Tom with a smile. "I mean, of course, The Garden Players." He lifted his cup. "I drink to you, my friends. To the sacrifice we make for our country. May God bless all of us in this great endeavor. Glory . . . and death!"

It seemed a very strange speech to be making just before a play—and a comedy at that. But the actors (apart from Florian) had all whispered a fervent "amen" and Tom joined them, not wishing to be left out. It still puzzled him, though, and he was about to ask Dr. Mobius what he had meant when there was a trumpet fanfare and a sudden murmur of voices on the other side of the screen.

At once the room began to fill up. Tom was forbidden to look around the screen, but he heard men and women talking, the clattering of shoes, the scrape of chairs being moved, and an occasional burst of laughter. Next to him Francis and Frances began to give their instruments a final tuning.

And then, as suddenly as it had started, the noise

stopped. There was a second fanfare and everyone in the room stood up. Tom still couldn't see anything, but he knew what had happened.

The queen had arrived.

The lights dimmed as most of the candles were blown out.

The audience took their places.

And the play began.

12

The Devil and His Boy

The play began with a prologue delivered by Dr. Mobius himself. Tom had heard it twenty or more times, but listening to it now from behind the screen he barely understood a word of it. It was as if there were a wind rushing through his ears. He couldn't hear anything. His mouth was dry. There was no feeling in his arms or legs.

He was, he realized, terrified. He was about to go on the stage in front of Queen Elizabeth and her court. He wondered if his legs would be able to move when his cue came. Not for the first time he wished he had never left Framlingham. Even life with the Slopes had been better than this.

Act 1, scene 1 began. Lucio had arrived in Venice. He had no money and nowhere to stay for the night. He called for his servant.

"Antonio! What ho? Antonio . . . !"

Tom stepped through the screen and onto the stage.

And the strange thing was, he left all his fear behind him. He had never felt such a transformation. It was as if he had stepped out of water onto dry land. Suddenly he was confident. He knew his lines. He knew what to do. It might have been Tom who had stood fearful and quivering behind the screen. But it was Antonio, servant of Lucio, who now began to talk, poking fun at his master and finally racing around the stage as he tried to escape a beating.

Tom didn't dare look into the shadows beyond the stage, but he could tell that the audience was enjoying the play. They had been silent throughout the prologue and the opening scene, but Tom's entrance had cheered them up. They laughed quite a few times, and when the scene ended they clapped.

Tom hurried off the stage. He wondered if the queen had applauded with them. The queen of England applauding him! But he didn't have time to think about it. The props were laid out on a table behind a fake wall—built for act 5—and he hurried over and picked up the two pitchforks.

He was halfway back to the stage before he knew something was wrong, and even then he wasn't sure what it was. At first he thought he had forgotten something. He had the pitchforks, the rope, the horns. What else was there? On the stage, Dr. Mobius was coming to the end of another soliloquy and Tom knew he had only moments before he had to go back on. He was wearing horns. He had put on his tail.

And then he saw what it was. The pitchforks were much too light. Being careful not to drop them, Tom turned them over in his hands and examined them. He quickly saw what had happened. The forks at the top were the same, but the long metal tubes had been replaced with lengths of wood. This made them much lighter to carry and easier to handle too. But Tom was surprised that Dr. Mobius should have changed them at this late stage and that he should have done so without telling him.

"Here comes Antonio now!"

Caught up with the pitchforks, Tom had almost missed his cue. He hurried onto the stage, almost dropping them as he went, and although Dr. Mobius glared at him, this got another laugh from the audience. The rest of the scene was a nightmare. Tom twisted one of his lines so it came out all wrong and completely forgot another. But try as he might, he found it almost impossible to concentrate. Ever since he had joined The Garden Players, all sorts of questions had been tapping at the window of his mind. He had tried to ignore them. But now, at the worst possible time, they had returned, louder and more insistent than ever.

Somehow he made it to the end of the scene, but

when he got backstage a furious Dr. Mobius—looking more devilish than ever—marched up and grabbed him.

"What are you doing?" he demanded in a hoarse whisper. His eyes were bulging with the effort of not shouting, and his makeup had begun to run.

"I'm sorry. . . ." On the other side of the screen Francis and Frances, the two musicians, were playing a duet.

Dr. Mobius closed his eyes, forcing himself to regain control. "Remember your lines," he said. "Concentrate!" He glared at Tom, then withdrew into the shadows.

Tom took a deep breath, angry with himself. Dr. Mobius was right. Whatever his doubts about the play, The Garden Players, and everything to do with them, he couldn't worry about them now. And what was so important about the pitchfork anyway? Once it had been metal. Now it was wood.

The pitchfork rolling across the deck. Florian diving and catching it. Dr. Mobius hitting him. "You idiot! You fool! . . . You almost lost it!"

Tom shook his head, forcing himself to forget it. Behind the screen the duet finished. The next scene began.

There were no further mishaps. Tom made no more mistakes, and an hour later he left the stage knowing that he would not be needed now until the very end of act 5.

It was the intermission. With the actors safely hidden behind the screen, the doors were opened and the audience retired for refreshments in another part of the palace. Tom was exhausted. Performing had sucked all the energy out of him. The other actors seemed as tired as he was. They also looked nervous, and this was surprising. The play was more than half over. The most difficult scenes were behind them. Why should they seem so nervous now?

Edmund Tilney—the master of the revels—had come backstage. The man with the scar came with him. Sir Richard seemed to have caught a cold. He was pale and sweating. "Her Majesty will be returning for the second half," Tilney said.

"We are honored." Dr. Mobius bowed low.

"Yes. You are." Tilney coughed dryly. "The play is too long and parts of it are rather dull. I would be grateful if you could shorten acts four and five. However, Her Majesty likes the boy—and the one playing the girl. She also likes the music. I take it there is more music?"

"Much more," Dr. Mobius assured him.

"Good." Tilney glanced at his clerk comptroller. "I must say, Sir Richard," he snapped, "this has not been one of your best recommendations."

He turned to leave, but Dr. Mobius stopped him. "Wait until the end of the performance before you pass judgement, my lord," he said. "I think I can promise you that it is a play that Her Majesty will not forget. Nor you either!"

Tilney raised his eyebrows at this, but said nothing. He left the room, Sir Richard hurrying after him.

Dr. Mobius and the other actors were sitting on benches, some lying on their back with their eyes closed. Florian was on his own, gnawing at his fingernails and staring into space. It was very dark behind the stage. Tom was glad about that. The darkness helped him think.

Someone had changed the pitchforks. Why? Back on the ship Dr. Mobius had almost killed him when he had dropped one of them. But why had the pitchforks been made of metal in the first place—and why metal tubes?

Metal tubes. For some reason that made Tom think of something. But what? Tom buried his head in his hands and searched through his memory. A metal tube, pointing at him. Of course! He was back in the wood with Hawkins. He was looking at Ratsey's gun.

There were guns in act 5 of *The Devil and His Boy* as well. Tom still hadn't solved the puzzle, but suddenly he was filled with dread. The master of the revels had checked the muskets himself. Tom remembered what Dr. Mobius had said.

"The barrels of the guns are fashioned from wood."

Moving slowly, trying to act as natural as possible, Tom went over to the artificial wall behind which the props were kept. He took one last look to make sure nobody was watching. Then he slipped behind the wall.

The muskets were lying in the right place, waiting for their appearance in act 5. They looked exactly the same as they had earlier that afternoon when Tilney had examined them, but even as he reached for the nearest one, Tom knew it had changed. Sure enough, it was heavier. He turned it around. The barrel of the gun was no longer made of wood. Nor was it solid.

And in that moment Tom knew everything.

It was very simple.

Dr. Mobius was planning to kill the queen! He was going to do it at the end of act 5 with muskets that—with the metal rods from the pitchforks screwed into place— were now *real* muskets. One shot for the queen. One shot for the guard by the door. Maybe Dr. Mobius and The Garden Players planned to fight their way out. But Tom had seen the fanatical light in Dr. Mobius's eyes. He had a job to do. He wouldn't care what happened to him when it was over.

Gently Tom lowered the musket back onto the table. What could he do?

He had to save the queen—but that might be easier said than done. How could he even leave the backstage area without the others seeing? And if he did manage to slip away, where could he go? Who could he tell? Sir Richard was obviously a traitor. What about Edmund

Tilney? But if he did speak out, would anyone believe him?

The problem was solved for him.

Tom hadn't heard anyone creeping around behind the wall, but the next moment something cold and hard crashed into the back of his neck. His legs buckled under him. The darkness came rushing in. He tried to fight it. But then Dr. Mobius hit him again and he was gone.

Tom woke up slowly with a pain in his head and a neck that felt as if it had been tied in a knot. He was lying underneath the table, his face pressed against the floor. He could taste straw and sawdust in his mouth. Even before he opened his eyes, he heard the play being performed in what seemed like the far distance. It took him a minute to make out the words and another minute to recall where they came from. Act 5, scene 2. Just a few pages until Lucio and Antonio were chased out of Venice by soldiers armed with . . .

He remembered the muskets and crawled painfully out from under the table. The muskets weren't there. He looked over to the side of the screen and saw Frederick and Philip, two of the actors, dressed as soldiers and carrying the muskets, waiting for their cue. He knew what was going to happen. In about one minute's time they would walk onto the stage. Nobody would even think of stopping them. They would raise their muskets, loaded and primed. There would be two explosions, and the audience probably wouldn't even realize what had taken place. Until they saw the queen's blood.

Tom had to stop them. He dragged himself to his feet, steadying himself with one hand on the table. Dr. Mobius must have believed he was dead. Certainly it was a miracle that whatever had hit him hadn't broken his neck. He took one step forward, then another. What should he do?

> *These merry devils must be banished hence.*
> *Go! Call the watch . . . !*

Tom knew the lines. The shooting was about to begin. There was no time to call out a warning. No time to try and explain.

Before he knew what he was doing, he was running—around behind the screen and out onto the stage. All the actors had their backs to him, so none of them saw him as he broke out into the light and kept on going. Tom just had time to glimpse Florian, turning his head toward him, his eyes widening, and next to him Dr. Mobius himself, his mouth half-open in midsentence. Tom had no real plan. All he knew was that he must put himself in front of the queen, protect her with his own body if he had to. Only seconds remained before Dr. Mobius would fire the first shot. Even now he might be taking aim.

Tom had reached the front of the stage. Everything

was a whirl. He opened his mouth to shout out a warning and at the same time he tried to position himself, spreading his arms to give the queen more cover. But it was then that his foot came down on a loose plank. The wood tilted and he lost his balance. With a great cry he pitched forward and, carried by his own momentum, plunged down onto the queen herself.

Then things didn't so much happen as explode. Tom fell on top of the queen, knocking her chair backward and sending her flying. There was a gasp of disbelief from the surrounding courtiers, screams from the ladies-in-waiting. Tom just caught sight of the queen's face, wide-eyed with shock. He was vaguely aware of black teeth and skin with too much makeup. To his horror, the queen seemed to be wearing a wig that had come loose. He tried to push himself away, but that just made things worse. To anyone looking, it must have seemed that he had grabbed hold of her as if trying to strangle her. Tom closed his eyes. He couldn't look. He didn't dare.

But even though it had all gone horribly wrong, he knew that he'd succeeded in what he'd set out to do. His attack had taken Dr. Mobius by surprise. Already the audience had closed in on the queen. The Gentlemen Pensioners were running forward from all sides to pull him off.

It didn't matter if Dr. Mobius had his musket ready or not. It was too late.

He had no clear shot.

Dr. Mobius did have a musket. He had snatched it from Frederick even as Tom ran past. Standing at the front of the stage, he waved it at the writhing, panicking mass that had been a courtly audience only seconds before. He caught sight of a stockinged leg, a jewelled foot, and fired. The sound of the explosion seemed huge, and suddenly the hall was filled with smoke and the smell of gunpowder. But the shot had missed. One of the courtiers had been hit in the back of his leg. With blood spurting from the wound, he cried out and fell to the ground.

The gunshot only added to the panic in the hall. Nobody knew quite where it had come from. All they knew was that one of the actors, the boy, had gone mad and thrown himself at the queen, and now somebody else had decided to join him. At least a dozen pairs of hands had grabbed Tom and he felt himself being ripped apart while, still underneath him, the queen had brought up her fist and was vigorously punching him on the nose and the stomach.

But at least some of the courtiers had kept their heads. The boy on top of the queen was an outrage. But now there was a musket somewhere in the room— and that was a deadly danger. Acting out of instinct, the courtiers had moved to surround the queen, forming a human wall for her protection. At the same time the

Gentlemen Pensioners had formed a front line, making for the stage.

Dr. Mobius knew he was finished. He grabbed the second musket and once again stared into the commotion. But now there was no sign of the queen at all. With a loud oath, he fired again, as if he could aim through so much writhing flesh and blood and still, miraculously, find his target. The second shot did get some way through. It hit Tom in the shoulder. He felt it slamming into his body, white-hot and furious. It was like the sting of some terrible insect. Tom screamed. At the same time he felt himself being plucked away. He opened his eyes and caught one last sight of the queen. It was as if she were being sucked into a tunnel in front of him. A fist hit him on the side of the face. Another hand tore at his hair. He was flung to the floor, his bones crashing into wood, and when he tried to move he found that he was pinned there, held down by at least five men.

Up on the stage the actors were trying to fight their way out. But the two muskets, with their single shots gone, were useless now, and the actors had no other weapons. It was all over very quickly. Only two of the actors—the two who had also played musical instruments—were killed. Later on it would be agreed that they had run onto the swords held up to stop them from leaving, preferring to kill themselves rather than face imprisonment, torture, and a more protracted death.

The queen had been helped to her feet and had disappeared with a swirl of silk. She was followed by bishops and courtiers, secret agents and councilors, already arguing among themselves, and by ladies-in-waiting who had turned into ladies-in-wailing as they sobbed in both terror and relief.

Someone rapped out an order, and Tom was scraped off the floor and lifted out of a puddle of his own blood. He stood, swaying on his feet. A couple of men supported him. He could never have stood on his own. Somehow he managed to bring his eyes into focus and saw Sir Richard, standing at the edge of the crowd. The clerk comptroller's face had gone completely white—all of it except for the scar that stood out, dark red and throbbing. His eyes were filled with terror.

But then another man, someone Tom had never seen before, pushed his way forward. This man was dressed in black and gray with a chain of office around his neck and a sword in his belt. The man had soft green eyes. His face was long and thin. "Who are you?" he asked.

Tom tried to answer. He opened his mouth, but nothing came out.

The man with green eyes looked at him more in puzzlement than in anger. "Why did you attempt this?" he asked.

"I didn't. . . ." It took all Tom's strength to whisper the two words, and even as he spoke them he knew it would be no good. Everyone in the room had seen what had happened. As far as they were concerned, he hadn't saved the queen. He had been the first to attack her! Whatever he tried to say now, nobody would believe him.

"Take him away!" the man said. "The others to the Tower for interrogation. This boy to Newgate. He has lain a hand on the most glorious person of Her Majesty. He has . . . *attacked* her! Such sacrilege is unheard of and we must ensure that no one does hear of it. Hang him tomorrow at first light. We'll learn from the others the reason for what happened here."

"Wait . . ." Tom began.

But already he was being dragged backward out of the Banqueting Hall. He felt the cold night air rushing over his shoulders, and its touch brought fresh pain from the wound in his back. There was a cart and a horse already waiting, and brutally, like a sack of meat, he was thrown into the back. Two guards climbed in with him. The horse was whipped forward.

Tom thought he was going to faint with the shock, the pain, the knowledge of what was to come. The night began to spin, but before he let it take him he forced his eyes open and looked out. They had just passed through the Holbein Gate. There were a few late-night revelers on the other side, making their way home with a servant—a linkboy—lighting their way. Tom lifted himself in the cart, and before his two guards could stop him, called out, "Find Moll Cutpurse! Tell her it wasn't me! Tell her that Tom—"

Then the guards reached him, grabbed him, and pulled him down, and Tom could say no more. Had the linkboy even heard him? Tom didn't know and he was too exhausted to care. He closed his eyes and drifted into sleep as the cart rattled on through the night.

13

On the Scaffold

It was seven o'clock in the morning and Gamaliel Ratsey was enjoying a healthy breakfast of hot porridge, bread, honey, and milk in the tavern where he had been staying since his arrival in London. The owners of the tavern had let him have his bed and breakfast at a special rate. In return Ratsey had promised not to kill them.

He looked up. Someone was standing over him, watching him with soft, attentive eyes. Automatically Ratsey's hand twitched for the hilt of his sword. Then he relaxed. It wasn't a man but a boy, and not a boy but a girl. He knew at once who it was.

"Moll Cut-throat!" he exclaimed. "You surprised me."

"It's Cutpurse," Moll sat down. "May I join you?"

"It seems you already have." Ratsey scooped up a mouthful of porridge. "Have you come to deliver the boy?"

"Not exactly." Moll gazed curiously at Ratsey as if trying to make him out. "I have something to tell you," she said.

"Go on." Ratsey gave her his best choirboy smile.

"Tom Falconer is in Newgate. He is to be hanged at eleven o'clock this morning."

Ratsey chuckled. "Is he, indeed? How do you know?"

"I heard last night."

Quickly Moll told Ratsey how she had been woken by the linkboy, and how at first light she had gone to Newgate Prison to find out what had taken place. Nobody had wanted to tell her anything, but she had bribed one of the guards with sixpence and heard the complete story from him.

"Tom is accused of trying to kill the queen," she told Ratsey now.

"That's ridiculous!"

"Of course it is. Tom would never try to kill anyone. All he wanted to do was act in a play. But these people he got involved with . . . they called themselves The Garden Players, but I've been asking around and nobody has heard of them—and from what Tom told me they weren't English."

"Maybe they were French."

"Or Dutch. Or Spanish. It doesn't matter. All that matters is that Tom can't have had anything to do with it. But he's going to hang in less than four hours if you and I don't do something."

"You and I?" Ratsey choked on his porridge. "You've taken leave of your senses! Why should I care if they hang the boy? They'll be doing me a favor."

"Is that your answer?"

"Yes. I always liked Tom. To be honest with you, I was never looking forward to murdering him. But what on earth makes you think I would wish to help him?"

This was the moment Moll had been dreading. She knew she'd taken a huge chance coming here. But she needed Ratsey's help and this was the only way. "I know who you are, Ratsey," she said. "But I also know who you used to be."

Ratsey's eyes narrowed. The smile faded from his lips. "What the devil are you talking about?" he asked.

"I'm talking about Captain Ratsey. The famous soldier who fought in the Irish campaigns and single-handedly captured the fort at Smerwick." She nodded gravely. "Oh, yes, I've heard all the stories about you," she went on. "People talk about Sir Francis Drake and Sir Walter Raleigh. But you could have been a bigger hero than either of them."

"Could have been! What do you mean 'could have been'! I *was* a bigger hero!" Ratsey threw down his spoon. "But that was a long time ago. Now I'm Ratsey the robber. Ratsey the killer. It's too late for me now."

"That's what I'm trying to tell you. This could be your last chance!" Moll reached out to take his arm, but Ratsey pulled it away. "People like us, Ratsey—pickpockets and highwaymen—what sort of life do we have? Always afraid. Always on the run. Until one day they catch up with us, and then . . ." Moll drew her hands to her throat. "But this is a chance to do one good thing. To be remembered as heroes. To make something of ourselves."

Ratsey fell silent. "So what are you suggesting, Moll Cut-price?" he demanded at length. "We just walk into Newgate and pull Tom out?"

"No. We go to Whitehall—to the queen."

"What? Old Queeny!"

"Yes. We'll tell her she's made a mistake. We'll make her listen to us. . . ."

"You think they'll even allow us in?"

"I know how to get us in, Ratsey. But I can't do it alone." Moll gripped his arm and this time he let her. "Doesn't Tom deserve a chance?" she said. "You said you liked him. Save his life and maybe you'll be saving your own. Think of what you were. Think of what you still can be."

Ratsey sighed. "My father always said I'd come to no good," he said. "He said I'd end up on the wrong end of a rope."

"So prove him wrong."

Ratsey thought for a long minute. He stuck a finger in his porridge and stirred it, then licked the finger. The porridge was cold. He sighed again. Then, finally, he saluted. "All right. All right. Captain Ratsey reporting for duty," he muttered. "Now tell me. What's the plan?"

There were fourteen prisons in London, but Newgate was the most feared. It was reserved for the very worst criminals and all of them arrived in the knowledge that they would not be staying long. Nine steps led to the way out—a rope and a trapdoor. Tom, however, was about to set the record for the shortest stay of all. And although the guards argued about this, they were fairly sure that he would be the youngest person they had ever hanged.

Tom awoke in a small, square cell, lying on a thin layer of straw with a tattered blanket half over his legs. A small, barred window—another square—looked out on gray sky and little else. He was not alone. A short, round man was lying on a bench, his knees tucked into his ample stomach, snoring loudly. Tom sat up. His shoulder, where he had been shot, still hurt dreadfully, and there was no movement at all in his right arm. He was filthy and his head ached.

The man on the bench grunted, sat up, and rubbed his eyes. Tom barely glanced at him, but the man gazed at Tom, shook his head, then—"My dear fellow!" he exclaimed. "It's John, is it not? No, it's not. It's Tim! No, it's not. It's Tom!" He smiled. "There have been so many boys. So many charming boys. I'm afraid I get a little hazy with names."

Now Tom recognized his cell-mate. The last time they had met, he had been interested in removing Tom's legs. The man was James Grimly. "What are you doing here?" Tom was so astonished that the words just tumbled out.

"A most serious misunderstanding with the authorities. They take a dim view, it would seem, of my . . . adjustments. Quite why, I cannot say. I feel London will be a much less cheerful place without Grimly's boys. Much less colorful. But there you are." He sighed. "One or two of my boys became rather ill," he admitted. "In fact, not to put too fine a point on it, they died. So now they've decided to adjust *me*." He ran a finger across his throat. "Permanently."

"They're going to hang me too," Tom said.

"My poor fellow! What did you do?"

Tom half-smiled. "They think I tried to kill the queen."

"Good lord!" Grimly blinked rapidly. "I have to say, Tom, I'm quite shocked. The queen!" He coughed, glanced at Tom, then looked away. "Mr. Bull should be in any time now," he said.

"Mr. Bull?"

"The hangman." Grimly smiled. "I'm sure he'll be delighted to meet up with you! Delighted, I'm absolutely sure."

The cart was old and piled high with loaves. As it rolled into Whitehall Palace, a couple of guards wandered over and glanced at the driver, a small, plump man who was also completely white—being covered from head to toe in flour.

"You come late!" one of the guards said.

"The oven went out," the driver—who was also the baker—replied. "The fool of a boy fell asleep in the night." The second guard was meanwhile searching underneath the cart. "What are you doing?" the driver exclaimed. "You know me well enough. What do you think I'm hiding?"

"We had some trouble here last night," the first guard explained. His partner straightened up and shook his head. "All right! Move on."

The cart continued around to the kitchen entrance. The driver looked left and right, then whistled softly. A moment later all the loaves heaved and separated as two figures, now as flour-covered as the driver, pulled themselves from under the pile.

"Thanks, Walter," Moll said.

"You owe me one for this, Moll," the baker muttered. He took a tray off the back. "Wait for the signal."

Moll Cutpurse and Gamaliel Ratsey looked a bizarre sight as they crept over to the kitchen entrance of Whitehall Palace: a girl in boys' clothes and a man in a mask, both of them bristling with weapons and covered in flour. Ratsey's mask was a small one and suited his name, for it was in the shape of a rat. Moll had tried to stop him from wearing it, but Ratsey had insisted. It was either with the mask or not at all.

The kitchen was heaving with cooks, under-cooks, waiters, and boys already hard at work on the midday meal. Half a deer was rotating slowly on a metal spit turned by a fat boy who was sweating as much as the meat he was cooking. Ratsey and Moll waited at the door as the baker went past them, calling out, "Fresh bread!" He walked over to the far side of the kitchen. Just as he reached the counter, he seemed to slip. The tray tipped and the rolls went everywhere. The baker yelled out and crashed to the ground, disappearing in a cloud of flour. At that moment, with all eyes on the baker, Moll and Ratsey slipped through the kitchen and out the other side.

They found themselves in a larder filled with cured hams, salted fish, and pickled vegetables. For a moment Moll thought they had walked into a closet, but there was a second door leading out and a moment later they found themselves in a long passage.

"Which way?" Ratsey whispered from behind his mask.

"Up!"

There was a staircase straight ahead of them, but before they could reach it a yeoman suddenly appeared, walking right toward them. Moll acted at once, grabbing him by the arm and swinging him around so that his back was to Ratsey. At the same time Ratsey lashed out, his fist catching the man in his neck. Moll caught him as he fell.

They reached the stairs and hurried up them. A second corridor led directly above the first, but this one was much more smartly decorated, with tapestries, curving wooden tables, and oil paintings.

"We must find the Presence Chamber," Ratsey said.

"Will the queen be there?"

"She might be. If she's not there, we can try the Watching Chamber; and if she's not there, she might be in the Great Hall."

"If she's not there, we're in trouble," Moll said.

And that was when the Gentlemen Pensioners appeared. Not just two or three, but an entire platoon on a routine patrol. They had stepped out of an archway at the end of the corridor, and now they were gazing at Moll and Ratsey with a mixture of astonishment and outrage.

"What was that about trouble?" Ratsey said.

"Back!" Moll shouted.

They turned and ran the way they had come, aware of the thunder of feet and the clatter of weapons behind them.

"In here!" Ratsey had reached another door and, grabbing hold of Moll, dragged her in.

They found themselves in a library, a room filled from floor to ceiling with precious books, many of them bound in gold and silver, some of them also decorated with pearls and precious stones. Two windows looked out on gardens and a tennis court, but there was no way to climb down. The room had only one door, and even as Ratsey slid a heavy chair across to block it, they heard the sound of the guards and the hammering of fists on wood. There was no way out. They were trapped.

Ratsey threw himself into the chair, adding his weight to the barrier, while Moll checked the windows, quickly returning with a shake of her head. Outside, the hammering stopped. The guards knew the intruders were trapped. All they had to do now was wait.

"Well, so much for that," Ratsey muttered. It was impossible to see his face behind the rat-mask, but he sounded only a little bit depressed. "No way out. . . ."

"Maybe we can explain . . ." Moll began.

"I wonder if we'll be hanged or drawn and quartered?" Ratsey mused. "I always wondered what that would be like. . . ."

Outside the door the hammering started again, but this time with some solid metal tool. A panel of wood splintered. An axe-head jutted through. Ratsey drew out his sword. Moll drew out hers. And then one of the bookshelves swung open and a man stepped into the room.

He was an old man, dressed in a black robe with a beard reaching down to his chest. Curiously, he was smiling. Even more curiously, he was holding a cat.

"Moll Cutpurse and Gamaliel Ratsey, I believe," he said. He spoke with a Welsh accent. "You had better come this way. I rather think the guards will be breaking in soon."

A second axe slammed into the door. Another panel of wood cracked open.

"Who are you?" Moll demanded.

"And where did you come from?" Ratsey asked.

"I fear we have no time for introductions," the old man said.

The door was struck twice more. One of its hinges shattered. Now they could hear the guards shouting in triumph.

"This way!" The old man gestured at the secret passage behind the bookshelf. Moll and Ratsey exchanged a glance, then ran forward. The old man and the cat followed them. The shelf of books swung shut behind them.

"Follow me," the old man said and, before they could argue, set off.

They were in a narrow passage lined with bricks on both sides and lit by a series of oil lamps. The passage seemed to run the entire length of the palace, with other passages and even staircases leading off. It was almost like a secret palace within the palace, a hidden network connecting every room in the building. The old man knew exactly where they were going. Humming softly to himself and still carrying the cat, he hurried on ahead, not even pausing to check that the other two were behind. At last he stopped beside a large panel of wood.

"This will lead you into the Presence Chamber," he said. "I cannot promise that the queen will be there. You may have scared her away with all the fuss. But you may still find what you want."

"Who are you?" Moll asked.

"My name is John Dee."

Ratsey was suspicious. "How did you know who we were? And why are you helping us?"

"Either we can spend all day talking or you can go in there and save the boy," Dee replied. He paused for a reply, but there was none. "I'll wish you a good day," he said.

"Good luck!"

Dr. Dee turned and walked away from Moll and Ratsey, heading back down the passage. For a moment neither of them spoke. Either they were going mad or the last words had just been spoken by the cat.

At length Moll laid a hand on the wooden panel and turned to Ratsey. "Are you ready?" she whispered.

"Yes."

"And I . . ." She pushed.

The Presence Chamber was full that morning. Privy councilors and clerks, gentlemen ushers and grooms, bishops and ambassadors. But even as Moll stumbled through a curtain and into the center of the darkly paneled room, she realized that she had failed. The throne was empty. There was no queen.

For a moment everyone froze. To the assembled courtiers it was as if two nightmare creatures—one with the face of a rat—had suddenly been conjured out of thin air. As Moll and Ratsey stood there, taking everything in, the spell was suddenly broken. Swords and knives were drawn. Doors crashed open and soldiers appeared, running forward and shouting. Ratsey had a knife in one hand and a sword in another. Moll also held a dagger. But it was useless. They were completely surrounded. And they were outnumbered by at least fifty to one.

"Put up your weapons!" someone exclaimed.

"This is the queen's Presence Chamber!"

"Traitors!"

Ratsey twisted around, his knife raised. "I'm not a traitor!" he said.

"We came to see the queen!" Moll cried, knowing it was useless. The guards were already moving in. She and Ratsey could kill one, two, three of them. But it wouldn't do any good. They would be cut down where they stood.

"Where did you come from?" A man who looked as if he was in charge had forced his way to the front of the circle. It was the man with green eyes who had spoken to Tom only the night before. "What do you want with Her Majesty?"

"To tell her she was wrong about Tom!"

"Who?"

"The boy! The boy who attacked her!"

"You know him? You're part of his company?"

"Yes—we know him. No—we're not with him."

The man with green eyes straightened up, his face suddenly grave. "Take them!" he snapped.

Before Ratsey and Moll could do anything, they were seized from behind. Their arms were wrenched back, their weapons falling uselessly to the ground. Ratsey's mask was torn off, along with Moll's hat. In seconds they were completely pinned down, unable to move.

"This is a mistake!" Moll shouted. "You don't understand. . . ."

"Take them to prison for interrogation," the man with the green eyes said. "And I want to know how they got in here!"

"Yes, Lord Moorfield." One of the guards bowed and signaled with his head. Moll and Ratsey were pulled backward out of the room.

They had almost reached the door before Moll remembered.

Sir William Hawkins. His last cry: "Go to Moorfield." Not a place! A person!

"Moorfield!" she cried out. "Tom is the boy you're looking for. The boy from Framlingham! He's the boy you sent Hawkins to find!"

But Moll was already out of the room.

The heavy door slammed shut as she and Ratsey were dragged away.

They knew when a hanging was going to take place. Just after eleven a hush descended on Newgate. The shouting of the prisoners, the mad laughter, the booming of doors, and the rattling of chains suddenly stopped and the corridors seemed empty, haunted. Then there was a groan as one door opened. And everyone knew. They had come for Tom Falconer.

Tom stood up as the door crashed open and Mr. Bull, the hangman, came in. He glanced first at James Grimly, who was cowering on the bunk with his head in his hands, then at Tom. "Good morning," he said. "I believe you and I have an appointment."

Tom nodded. The hangman wasn't at all what he

had expected. Mr. Bull was a small, neat man dressed in a blue velvet tunic. He gestured with one hand and four guards marched in to surround Tom. "This won't take a minute," he said.

One of the guards grabbed Tom's arms and, ignoring his wound, tied his hands behind his back. Then, with Mr. Bull at the front and the guards on all four sides, Tom was led down a corridor, past a series of barred doors. The corridor was arched, the brickwork ancient and blood-red. The straw under his feet was filthy, but Tom couldn't smell it. He couldn't hear anything. All his senses seemed to be failing him . . . even his sight. The darkness seemed to be rushing in.

They walked to the end of the corridor and down a staircase carved out of stone. Tom had thought they would be going outside the prison, but the stairs led to another corridor and then to a final archway. The scaffold stood in a room at the far end.

The strange thing was, Tom wasn't afraid. He was amazed. The scaffold was just how he had always imagined it. It was exactly the same as the drawings he had seen schoolboys make in Framlingham: three pieces of wood, a trapdoor with a lever, and, hanging over it, a noose. As simple as that.

The scaffold had been erected in a great chamber closed to the outside world apart from a series of small windows set too high up to see through. The chamber was shaped like the dome of a cathedral, the walls made of bare brick. The size of the place made the scaffold seem small and insignificant.

Mr. Bull coughed discreetly and the party moved forward. Nine steps—Tom could count them now. He reached the first and stumbled. With his hands tied behind him and unable to balance himself, he might have fallen, but one of the guards reached out and steadied him. He began to climb.

As he took the first step, a figure appeared from underneath the scaffold. This was a huge man, bare-chested, with a black hood over his face. Tom glanced inquiringly at Mr. Bull, who shook his head. Tom understood. Mr. Bull organized the business. He was, if you like, the artist. But the actual work itself, that had to be left to a hired hand.

Tom reached the top of the scaffold and stood in the middle of the platform. He could just make out the cracks of the trapdoor that would open when the lever was pulled. The wooden planks creaked slightly underneath him. He tried to swallow, but his mouth was too dry. The hooded man had followed him up and leaned forward to pull the noose around his head. For a moment his arms, and the huge muscles of his chest, were close to Tom's face. Tom caught the slightly bitter smell of the man's sweat. He jerked away and felt the touch of the rope around his neck. It was hairy and tickled.

Tom hadn't seen any drummers, but suddenly the chamber was filled with a steady drumming, starting low but rising in volume as the beat got faster. He had expected a blindfold, but none had been offered. What should he look at? What would be the last thing he ever saw? He tried to concentrate his sight on the daylight streaming in through the upper windows, but out of the corner of his eye he could see the hooded man reach for the lever.

Tom closed his eyes.

Mr. Bull nodded. The hooded man's hand tightened. "Stop!"

It was a woman's voice, loud and authoritative, the sort of voice that had to be obeyed. The single word had come from the door, but it seemed to explode in the chamber, echoing off the walls. The drumming stopped instantly. The hooded man, Mr. Bull, and the four guards fell to their knees. Tom slowly turned his head, the noose rubbing against his neck.

Queen Elizabeth swept into the room, and she had never looked more awesome or more majestic. She was wearing a billowing dress of black satin decorated with gold buckles rising all the way up the front to her neck. Her face was surrounded by a collar of dazzling white with a great band of white pearls hanging from her neck. She had come to a halt in a circle of light lancing down from one of the windows, and in the dark interior she seemed to burn gold and white and every color of the spectrum. Her eyes burned brightest of all. And they were staring at Tom.

"Bring the boy down," she said.

For a moment nobody moved. Then everyone ran for the steps, fighting to be the first to reach the boy who was now dangling from the rope, having fainted where he stood.

14

Five Heads

The queen came to see Tom a few days later.

He had been taken to the Tower, not to one of the prisons but to a comfortable room overlooking the Thames. As soon as he had been strong enough to walk, he had tried the door and had been pleased to discover that it wasn't locked. There had been other surprises. The room had a bed with sheets of pure linen. And Tom had been brought clothes that were finer and more expensive than anything he had ever seen. He had been given wonderful food served on a solid silver plate.

And now, here was the queen of England, standing in his room. Just the two of them. Alone.

Impossible!

Tom bowed low, fixing his eyes on the floor. He heard the queen sweep into the room and sit down on a chair. After a long silence, wondering if he dared, Tom looked up.

"They call you Tom Falconer," the queen said.

"Yes, Your Majesty."

"Tom . . ." The queen was staring at him with a whole range of contrary emotions in her eyes. She seemed happy and sad, angry and pleased, aloof but uncertain, royal and yet somehow afraid. It was late in the afternoon. The sun was beginning to set. The Thames was flowing from silver to a burning red. "Sit down, Tom," the queen said.

There was only one chair in the room. Tom sat down on the bed.

"How is your wound, child?"

"Much better, thank you, Your Majesty." His wound had been cleaned and bandaged. It was hurting now—a sure sign that it was beginning to heal.

The queen bowed her head.

"I have done you great wrong," she said.

"No, Your Majesty. You're not to blame. . . ."

The queen waved a hand to silence him. Sitting on the chair, just a few inches away, she looked much more like the old woman that she undoubtedly was. Her skin was heavily made-up, but Tom could still see the wrinkles. He already knew (although it shamed him to remember) that her bright red hair was a wig. Her teeth were entirely black. And yet her pale skin and bright blue eyes reminded him of someone. He wondered who.

"I have to talk to you about . . . other matters, Tom," the queen said. "But I might as well begin with Dr. Mobius and The Garden Players." She paused. "As I am sure you have guessed, they were not an acting company at all. In fact, they were Spanish, members of a secret organization that calls itself the Garduna. They intended to kill me, even though they knew they would all die themselves. And they would have succeeded, had it not been for you."

She smiled. "I know now—at least, I believe I have guessed—exactly what you were doing that night. You were trying to protect me. Am I right?"

"Yes, Your Majesty." Tom hung his head in shame. "I didn't mean to embarrass you."

"I have done much, much worse to you, child. But I will come to that soon. As you probably know, the man who calls himself Dr. Mobius had bribed one of my officers. Sir Richard Brooke."

"The man with the scar!"

"A man who will have more than a scar by the time I have finished with him! He worked for my lord chamberlain. Between them they choose which plays I see. Sir Richard was paid well to introduce The Garden Players. But soon it will be his turn to pay."

"How did you find out, Your Majesty?" Tom asked. He was slowly getting used to the fact that he was having a quiet chat with the richest and most powerful woman in the world. He was even beginning to enjoy it. "How did you find out that I was not on their side?"

"You have your two friends to thank for that."

"Two . . . ?"

"Moll Cutpurse and Gamaliel Ratsey."

"What?" Ratsey had *helped* him? The very thought made Tom's head spin.

"They broke into my Presence Chamber, and although I had already retired, they had the good fortune to come upon one of my spies. A man by the name of Henry Moorfield."

"Moorfield?" Tom gasped. "I thought it was a place!"

"You were told to go to Moorfield by Sir William Hawkins. I know. And this is where it gets difficult, Tom. This is where it finishes and where it starts."

There was a long silence. Then, to Tom's astonishment, the queen got off the chair and sat down next to him on the bed. Gently, she laid her hands on his face, one underneath his chin and one on the side of his cheek, and turned him so that she could look into his eyes. At the same time Tom looked into her eyes—he couldn't avoid it—and saw how sad they had become.

"Listen to me," she said, and her voice was a whisper. "You must never tell anyone else what I am going to tell you. Believe me, Tom. It is a secret that could destroy us both."

She paused again. Then . . .

"More than forty years ago, when I was just sixteen years old, I made a dreadful mistake. My father had died and the king—Edward—was only a boy, younger than you.

"He was too young to reign on his own, so the council elected a man to look after him—a protector. That man was called Edward Seymour. And the mistake I made was to fall in love with his brother.

"Thomas Seymour—yes, he had the same name as you—was a rogue and a ruffian and a fool. But he was also handsome and brave, and he made me laugh. He was much older than me and he was married, but . . . well, one thing led to another and he—" she found it difficult to frame the words—"he left me with a child!

"Those were dangerous times, Tom. The day I learned I was pregnant, Thomas Seymour was arrested—for treason." She sighed. "He was no more a traitor than I was, but as I told you, he was a fool, and two months later he lost his head. And there was I, left behind, carrying his child! If anyone had found out, Tom, believe me, my head would have gone too. As it was, I was sent here, to the Tower, and interrogated. Luckily I kept my head. And my secret. But it was close.

"I left the Tower and went to Hatfield, and it was there, in complete secrecy, that I gave birth to a child, a boy. I called him Thomas, after his father, but I saw him for only one day. It was too dangerous to keep him close. It hurt me, but I knew I had no choice. A servant of mine had the baby passed to a wet-nurse and smuggled away. He was taken to a family in Suffolk who agreed to adopt him. They also changed his name. They called him Robert."

Tom stared. He couldn't believe what he was hearing. And he was already beginning to see what was about to come.

"After I lost the child, I thought about him every hour of every day," the queen went on. "But then a time came when I had to force myself to forget him, to pretend that he did not exist." She sighed. "It was difficult staying queen. And it's still murderously difficult being queen. And admitting to having an illegitimate child by a man executed for treason forty-four years ago would only make it all more difficult. I have had no choice. I have had to forget my own child."

"What happened to him?" Tom asked. But he already knew.

"Something went wrong. The family that was supposed to be looking after him failed me. Thomas—or Robert as he now was—grew up to become the falcon keeper at Framlingham Castle. But then there was an accident. He fell off a horse. . . ."

"You're speaking of my father," Tom said.

"Yes."

There was another long silence.

"You're my grandmother," Tom said.

"Yes." The queen took Tom's hand in her own, holding it as if it were a precious object rather than flesh and blood. "I never knew your father had died. And I never knew that you had been born," she said. "Not until recently."

"And so you sent Sir William Hawkins to find me?"

"Yes. He did not know who you really were, although he may have guessed. He was a spy. He was clever."

"You know how he died?"

"Yes. We managed to get the truth out of that scoundrel Ratsey, and believe me, Tom, he should lose his head for his part in all this. But, well, we can discuss that later."

The queen stood up. "I will return this evening," she said. "Then we can talk again."

"Wait a minute!" It suddenly occurred to Tom that he had completely dropped the "Your Majesty." And he had just told the queen what to do! "I beg your pardon, Your Majesty," he went on, "but there is one thing." He paused to collect his thoughts. "You told me that nobody must know. So what you're saying is, I'm your grandson. But I'm not going to be king."

"The question of who will be king is something the whole country has been asking," the queen replied. "And I wish Parliament would stop bothering me about it. I could introduce you, if you wanted, Tom. And maybe the people might accept you. On the other hand, it could lead to a bloody civil war." She shrugged. "Do you want to be king?"

"I don't think so," Tom said.

"Well, I can see you've inherited a little common sense," the queen said. She hesitated, suddenly serious. "But consider this, Tom. I can help you become whatever you want. Think about it. We will meet again this evening."

That evening Tom and the queen met for the last time.

"I want to ask you a favor," Tom said.

"Go on."

"I've been thinking about Florian. He was one of The Garden Players. Have you . . . ?" Tom hesitated to say it.

"He hasn't been executed, Tom. Not yet."

"Will you spare him, Your Majesty?" Tom blushed without quite knowing why. "I know he was part of it, but I don't think he wanted to be. Dr. Mobius was his uncle. He just did what he was told. The same as me when I was at The Pig's Head."

The queen didn't look pleased. "It is never a good idea to spare your enemies," she said, "because it gives all your other enemies ideas." She softened. "But if you really think he was forced into it, I could just have him tortured. . . ."

"Couldn't you just let him go?"

"If you insist. Is there anything else?"

Tom smiled. "I was wondering about Moll and Ratsey. . . ."

"Two vagabonds! A pickpocket and a highwayman. I have to say, Tom, for someone with royal blood, you've been keeping some pretty low company. But you are alive and I have them to thank for it. What do you want me to do with them? Don't tell me you want me to knight them!"

"Will you let them go?"

"I already have. Mistress Cutpurse left with a bag of gold for her pains."

"What about Ratsey?"

"He was lucky to escape with his life." Suddenly the queen was stern. "Maybe he was not entirely to blame for what he became, Tom. And every man deserves a second chance. But I tell you this. If he ever ends up on one of my scaffolds—and I'm certain he will—I won't be there to help."

"I understand."

The queen sat next to Tom once again and held him in her arms. "But what of you, Tom? Have you thought of your own future? I can give you a house and land. I can make you a lord. . . ."

"I don't want to be a lord, Your Majesty." Tom smiled. "I want to be an actor!"

"What?"

"There's a man I met. His name is William Shakespeare."

The queen nodded. "Yes. I have heard of him. I hear he's rather good."

"I met him when I was trying to get into the Rose Theatre. We got on quite well and I'm sure he'd help me if . . ."

"I'm not sure I approve of players," the queen said. "They're a rowdy lot at the best of times. But if you're sure that's what you really want. . . ."

"It is. More than anything in the world."

"I will have a word with Master Shakespeare." She stood up and once again she was sad. "I think it would be easier for both of us if we kept ourselves apart," she said. "But if you ever need my help, Tom, I am very easy to find."

"I'm sure, Your Majesty."

"And if you can't be my grandson, you can still be my friend. After all, you did save my life."

"I'll always be your servant." Tom bowed.

The queen turned and left the room.

A few weeks later rehearsals began for a new play that was to be performed at the Rose Theatre in the early spring. The play was called *Romeo and Juliet*. It was a love story.

Tom only had a small part in the play. He had been cast as a servant, and he only had a few lines. But it was a start. And what mattered to him was that he was an actor, an official member of the Company of Admiral's Men.

He had only seen Moll once since winter had ended. She had come to the theatre to wish him luck and had stayed just long enough to pickpocket a couple of spectators before heading off to a thieves' dinner-and-dance in Shoreditch. Gamaliel Ratsey had gone straight back to Suffolk without bothering to say good-bye. Tom had to admit he was rather glad. The trouble with Ratsey was that you never knew if he was going to shake your hand or cut your throat.

"Tom!" Shakespeare was calling him now, a great pile of papers in one hand, a feather quill in the other. The two of them spent much of their time together. Tom loved giving Shakespeare ideas for new plays. In return Shakespeare was teaching Tom how to read.

Tom hurried over to join his friend.

At the same time, a short way up the Thames, four men and one woman were gazing in Tom's direction, as if trying to see what he was doing. Dr. Mobius was the first of them. Then came James Grimly, Sir Richard Brooke, and finally Sebastian and Henrietta Slope. They were almost unrecognizable by now, as they'd been there for several weeks. Five heads on five spikes high above London Bridge.

Beneath them, the river flowed gently past, the water glistening in the dying light.

> *Good night, good night!*
> *Parting is such sweet sorrow,*
> *That I shall say good night*
> *till it be morrow. . . .*

Afterword

This is the chapter you don't have to read.

But for those who might want to know, a lot of *The Devil and His Boy* is based on facts. Many of the characters, for example, were alive in 1593. Elizabeth I and Shakespeare, of course, but also Gamaliel Ratsey, Moll Cutpurse, Philip Henslowe, Lord Strange (who really did like acrobats), Edmund Tilney (master of the revels), Dr. John Dee, and even Mr. Bull, the hangman.

I have tried to describe London exactly as it was in the sixteenth century—or at least, exactly as we think it was. Paul's Walk really was at the heart of the city—it was the place where people went to find work—and there was an open area called Moorfield just north of Moorgate. The Rose Theatre, Newgate Prison, and Whitehall were all much as I've described, and the Banqueting Hall really was made of cloth (it was replaced with a solid structure in the reign of King James). Framlingham is also a real town. You can still visit the castle with its peculiar, twisted chimneys. Even now nobody is sure why they were built.

The only thing in this book that is definitely not accurate is the language spoken by the characters. Elizabethans did have a different way of saying things, and if I had imitated their dialogue, it would have made the book seem very old-fashioned at best—and at worst completely incomprehensible. I have, however, tried not to make the language seem too brash and modern. For example, I've avoided modern slang!

As to the events described in this book . . .

It is certainly true that the young Elizabeth had a close relationship with Thomas Seymour, brother of the protector. It was also rumored that she carried his child. Elizabeth herself wrote, "that there goeth rumours abroad which be greatly both against my honour and honesty (which above all things I esteem) which be these: that I am in the Tower and with child by my lord Admiral. . . ."

There were also many people who hated the queen and wanted her dead—mainly the Spanish. The Garduna was a secret organization closely linked with the Inquisition. They were also known as the Holy Warriors of Spain.

Moll Cutpurse was a famous thief of the sixteenth

century. She is even the subject of a play—*The Roaring Girl*. Moll did dress up in boys' clothes. She was involved with a "school for crime." And she was the daughter of a shoemaker. It's nice to know that she lived until she was seventy, a remarkable age, before she died of dropsy.

Gamaliel Ratsey was less fortunate. The most famous highwayman of his time, Ratsey did have noble parents and had served in Ireland before he took to crime (many thieves were unemployed soldiers). He was also well known for his horrible masks. Sadly, eight years after this book ends, Ratsey was betrayed by a friend and taken prisoner. He was hanged.

John Dee is an interesting character. He was Queen Elizabeth's personal magician, a Welshman who spent much of his life searching for the secret of how to turn metal into gold. Dee also owned a "stone of vision"—I didn't make it up. There's no record, however, of his owning a talking cat.

Wherever possible in *The Devil and His Boy* I've tried to use actual details from the sixteenth century to give the story a ring of truth. Queen Elizabeth *did* have five quilts on her bed. Dinner at The Pig's Head would have cost you "sixpence downstairs and eightpence up." London boys did enjoy throwing mud-balls at strangers. And so on.

That said, however, it is quite possible that teachers will find some mistakes in this book. These mistakes are entirely deliberate. I put them in to keep the teachers happy.

Anthony Horowitz